ALMOST
HUMAN

ALMOST HUMAN

HC DENHAM

Matador
9 Priory Business Park,
Wistow Road, Kibworth Beauchamp,
Leicestershire. LE8 0RX
Tel: 0116 279 2299
Email: books@troubador.co.uk
Web: www.troubador.co.uk/matador
Twitter: @matadorbooks

ISBN 978 1838596 125

British Library Cataloguing in Publication Data.
A catalogue record for this book is available from the British Library.

Printed and bound in Great Britain by 4edge Limited
Typeset in 11pt Adobe Jenson Pro by Troubador Publishing Ltd, Leicester, UK

Matador is an imprint of Troubador Publishing Ltd

To my patient and encouraging partner (in all things).

*"That man is best
who sees the truth himself."*

HESIOD, GREEK PHILOSOPHER POET, 700 BC

CHAPTER
ONE

"How are you both settling in?"

Derek Boyd looked past Trenhaile's head to a vast panoramic window where a line of robots could be seen moving ant-like across a featureless plain. He was a biologist, not an engineer, and he couldn't help finding robots slightly sinister, particularly in large numbers. He looked back at Trenhaile, who was smiling blandly at him across the coffee table. *Smug*, he thought. Boyd was unused to discussing personal matters with strangers – or indeed with anyone.

"Well, to be honest, Sheila's finding it hard." Boyd shifted uncomfortably in his chair. "You see, she had a career in the UK. She was a college lecturer – and of course we had lived in Finchley for a number of years, so we had a good circle of friends. I'm out so much – well, she's lonely, I guess – and at a bit of a loose end. I'm not very good at dealing with this sort of thing. If there was a practical solution, I could take some action, but as it is…" He trailed off.

"Of course, there aren't many non-working partners out here – so we are a bit short on what I might term 'extra-mural activities', painting clubs and so forth, although we do our best here at Camp Zebra. There is the bar, and the games room." Trenhaile smiled again. *Patronising*, was Boyd's thought.

Trenhaile's whole appearance irritated him – the stylish lightweight suit, the laundered white shirt, tieless and open at the neck, of course, just to show he was 'modern'. Boyd himself never wore either suits or ties – his clothes were strictly functional. Ridiculous in this climate – suits. The other intensely irritating feature of Trenhaile was his flourishing head of dark hair. *He can't be much younger than me*, thought Boyd, who had settled for a close crop of his remaining strands several years earlier.

"Of course, people do sometimes take a bit of time to settle in," Trenhaile went on, "and, quite frankly, a lot of partners prefer to stay at home for the duration. That can be hard on the relationship in another way, of course."

Boyd's discomfort seemed to increase. "She was determined to come out here – there were reasons." He wasn't going to go into those with Trenhaile.

"Perhaps we could arrange for her to help out a bit with some admin – well below her capabilities, I'm sure, but it would help to fill the days, and I'm confident I could arrange something like that." Trenhaile leaned back in his chair and fiddled with the pens on his desk, managing in the process to sneak a surreptitious look at his watch.

"I don't think that would do it. It's become quite a serious issue." Boyd looked even more uncomfortable. "I think there may be a touch of actual clinical depression. She's become quite paranoid – afraid to be alone in the house – I am away overnight quite a lot, sometimes a week at a time at the pods. She seems to have a nervousness of robots – inconvenient, considering the fact that the base is run by them!"

"Very," said Trenhaile drily. "People have got to face it. Robots are the future. URC is based on that premise – robots and your field of activity – 'making the desert bloom', as you put it in your part of the prospectus."

Was there a slight sneer in the last remark? Boyd wondered. "I know I'm privileged to be involved in this project and Sheila is right with me on that. She wants to stay, but her state of mind is quite worrying – and there are robots everywhere – so the phobia is confining her to the house. And… I've had to get rid of the cleanbot." Boyd's tone clearly demonstrated his irritation with his wife.

"Pity," said Trenhaile, "I find mine an absolute boon." And the bland smile again. "You don't have to make it tea or stop to chat."

There was no answering smile from Boyd at this remark, and Trenhaile started to feel a little sorry for the rather faded, balding little man in front of him. He was also, though, suppressing a feeling of annoyance at being confronted with the sort of personal problem that in his view would not arise if people took rational decisions. However, it was his job to ensure that personal problems did not interfere with the productivity of the workforce. He leaned forward, an expression of earnestness on his face.

"I can see that this is a serious worry for you and, of course, you're likely to be here for some time. It's our job in human resources to try and iron out any little problems our colleagues may have." He paused thoughtfully. "I think I may have a possible solution. Let me run it by you."

CHAPTER
TWO

Hughie arrived at the Boyds' apartment a week later. Trenhaile had explained that the HU5 robots had not been designed to look human.

"We tried prototypes with humanoid features and skin and some people react badly to them – find them, I think, a little sinister. So I'm suggesting you try an HU5. They have some physical human characteristics – size, shape, a suggestion of facial features – but they're very clearly robots. In their interactions with humans, though, the empathy and reaction to human emotions, they're really very human – well, probably superior to most humans – super-human, you might say!" with a laugh. "They have no ego, for one thing – they have no agenda of their own, endless patience."

Indeed, when the Boyds' HU5 – 'Hughie', as he had been named by the technicians, arrived, he was so clearly a robot that it was touch and go as to whether Sheila would let him into the apartment. Boyd was with her and managed to persuade her to sit down while the handler led Hughie into the room. He had a metallic skin, but his limbs moved flexibly – rather more smoothly than most humans – and he had a face with eyes and a sketchy nose. His voice, however, when it came, seemed to come from deep inside his body, and his sculpted mouth didn't move. His lidless eyes were back-lit a soft grey.

He took a seat opposite Sheila and introduced himself in the gentlest of voices.

Later on, while Hughie busied himself in the kitchen, Boyd followed Sheila into the bedroom to find her, as so often recently, in tears.

"I can't stand it. You think you can fob me off with a piece of machinery." She buried her head in her hands.

Boyd stood awkwardly beside the bed. "I don't know what you want," he said, with more than a hint of exasperation in his voice. "You wanted to come – you know how important my work is. This robot will take all the dull tasks off you, look after you while I'm away – and, so they say, be company if you want it. This is your chance to get on with your painting."

She turned to him in despair. "You've become so distant – I just, I just want some affection… some of *you*. Hold me… please."

He came over to the bed and put his arms round her, but his thoughts were already elsewhere.

"Look – I've got to go back to the lab. Have a rest – and then go back out and try to get to know Hughie. The guys would like a report on him. He's a prototype – never been put in a real domestic situation before. It can be a project for you to monitor how useful he is. They'd like you to keep a diary."

She sat up on the bed and turned away from him. With her back to him she said, dully, "OK – I'll have a rest and then I'll try. I don't like robots, but he doesn't make me feel as uneasy as some of the others. I don't know why I'm calling him 'he' – he's just a machine."

Boyd sounded relieved. "That's better – I'll be back late, so just leave something on the side for me and I'll heat it up when I get back. You're meant to think of Hughie as a 'he' – that's part of the point. He's a companion as well as a machine." As he said it Boyd was struck by the strangeness of his own remark, but as soon as he was out of the door, the thought vanished.

When Boyd got back late that night, he was surprised to find all the lights on. It was clear that Sheila had not gone early to bed with a sleeping pill as had been her recent habit. She had set her easel up in the corner of the living room next to the large picture window and was engrossed in a canvas. Hughie was sitting at her side next to her paint tray with a palette in his hand. He appeared to have been mixing paint.

He rose at Boyd's entry and greeted him.

"Can I get you some tea or coffee, sir? Or perhaps you would prefer something stronger to drink? There are some sandwiches in the kitchen; should I bring them for you?"

Used to entering an empty living room and rather disconcerted at an unfamiliar presence in his house, albeit a mechanical one, Boyd said rather gruffly that he would help himself and went into the kitchen.

As he sat at the breakfast bar with a beer eating his sandwich, he could hear Sheila and Hughie talking quietly to each other, apparently absorbed in the joint activity. He realised that Sheila had not greeted him when he arrived.

On returning to the living room, he went over to Sheila – Hughie tactfully withdrawing to another part of the room – and noted with pleasure that she was working on a canvas she had started before they left the UK. This seemed to him to be a tremendously good sign.

"So pleased you decided to go back to that one. I thought you'd really got something there."

Sheila leaned back from the easel and said, rather abstractedly, "Yes, it just came to me as I was telling Hughie about London, that I might be able to finish it now. Somehow, recollecting it from a distance helped me to see how I might be able to get the essence of it, if you understand what I mean."

Boyd was far from understanding her meaning but so delighted not to be met with a mask of frozen misery that he was certainly not going to say so.

It seemed an odd thing to do, but Trenhaile had advised him to interact with Hughie as if he was a person, since that was the way that his program would learn to respond appropriately to the individuals with whom he was placed.

He had been pre-programmed with a considerable amount of background data provided by Boyd, but he would develop in response to the needs and situations he encountered. So Boyd turned to Hughie and said with what he couldn't help feeling to be a degree of forced joviality,

"You'd be fascinated by London, Hughie. It's such an exciting and varied city – so different from this camp and its surroundings. Sheila's painting might give you a feel for it."

"I would very much like to see London, sir." Hughie's reply was mellifluous and deferential. "My experience to date has, of course, been very limited."

"Do call me Derek," said Boyd, with some embarrassment. "I'm so pleased you've been able to help Sheila. She used to paint a lot in her spare time, but she's found it hard to get going since she's been here."

He stood for a few minutes, uncertain as to what to say next. Sheila remained poised with her paintbrush in hand and her head half turned towards Boyd, but apparently not ready to resume her work. Hughie, still holding the palette, remained standing beside the chair he had been sitting on.

"I think I'll turn in," said Boyd rather awkwardly. "If you're going to be very late, Sheila, could you go into the spare room? I've got an early start. We're off to check the plantations up north. I may be away overnight, so I need to pack a bag as well."

"That's fine," said Sheila, turning back to the easel. "Take care." And she leaned towards the canvas. Hughie sat down again and bent towards her. As he went into the bedroom, Boyd could hear them talking quietly.

CHAPTER
THREE

Boyd's trip to Camp Greenhouse, the site of the main experiment, took longer than he had expected. He and his team had found that the pods created to protect the embryonic crops had been damaged and they had had to stay on site until the technicians had arrived to repair the damage, so he was actually away for a week.

Boyd loved his work – "obsessive" was Sheila's description of his attitude – but he kept in contact with her electronically as much as possible when away in the field. When he had contacted her on this trip, he had been relieved to note that Sheila had appeared calm and untroubled by his absence whereas, in the past, any prolonged period of absence on his part had tended to produce what Boyd would describe to himself as an extreme, if not hysterical, reaction. *The robot appeared to be fulfilling its function*, Boyd told himself with satisfaction. He could get on with his work without having to worry about his wife's state of mind.

He and his team arrived back at Camp Zebra late at night. As she had not seemed concerned at his absence, Boyd hadn't bothered to let Sheila know that he was due to arrive. Feeling dead tired but immensely satisfied with his team's achievements, Boyd let himself quietly back into the flat. He was not surprised to find it in darkness – Sheila had clearly gone to bed. Her easel and paints stood in the corner, and it was clear that she'd been working. There was an unfinished canvas on the easel and a completed one propped against the wall. He never attempted to understand or judge art, but he was pleased to see this evidence of productivity.

The living room was empty, so he went into the spare room to leave his things and then into the kitchen to make himself a hot drink. Standing over the sink, it suddenly occurred to him to wonder where Hughie was. Surely he couldn't be in the bathroom. And then, reflected in the black viscosity of the kitchen window, Boyd saw the door to the main bedroom open and Hughie glide silently out. Boyd was so surprised he said nothing as Hughie came towards him and stood in the kitchen doorway.

"Please let me do that for you, Derek. You must be tired after your journey."

Boyd, who found having the robot behind him unsettling, turned quickly and said abruptly, "There's no need, Hughie. I can do it myself. Is Mrs Boyd in bed?"

Boyd looked straight into the enigma of Hughie's grey eyes.

"Sheila has been working hard on her painting, Derek. She was tired, and I don't believe she knew you were coming home tonight."

"No – that's true. We weren't sure when the technicians would arrive," said Boyd gruffly. He was irritated at Hughie's use of his and Sheila's first names but, as it had been his own suggestion, he could hardly go back on it without appearing erratic.

"Can I unpack for you while you relax, Derek?"

"No, thank you, Hughie." Boyd was annoyed with himself for feeling uncomfortable. This was a machine, after all, so why was he feeling as if a stranger had infiltrated his home? Of course, Hughie was designed to mimic human responses, that was the point of him, but Boyd was a scientist and should be able to react rationally to his presence. "There's no need to keep you, Hughie – I'm not going to need you tonight – nor, I should imagine will Mrs Boyd, Sheila, as she's in bed."

"Of course, Derek." Hughie's exit was so silent and unobtrusive that, although Boyd watched him go, he seemed to melt out of sight. By the time Boyd followed him out into the living room it was empty. Before he could relax, Boyd needed to know where Hughie had gone. He found him in the garage upright against the back wall, a disconcerting blankness replacing the luminosity of his grey eyes.

For no reason he could have explained to himself, Boyd locked the connecting door to the garage before going to bed in the spare room.

He was woken the next morning by Sheila bringing him a cup of tea.

She sat on the bed and chatted happily to him while he drank it. He hadn't seen her so relaxed since their arrival at the camp.

"I've really got going with my painting again. Did you see the canvas by the wall? I'm quite pleased with it. Anyway, how was the trip? Did you manage to sort out the problems?"

Normally Boyd would have been pleased, both at Sheila's upbeat mood and at any show of interest in his work, which she often seemed to regard as an enemy, but on this occasion he had a nagging concern.

"I thought I wouldn't disturb you when I got back. Hughie told me you were asleep." Was it his imagination or was there a touch of evasiveness in her manner?

"Well, actually, I've been working non-stop since you left and I tend to be dropping by about 9.30 – I was dead to the world."

It was awkward, but Boyd had to say it. "Hughie was in your room when I arrived. Are you OK with that when you're asleep?"

Sheila looked away for a moment. "I think he was probably just tidying up my things. He's so quiet, he doesn't disturb me at all."

"Well, I don't want him coming in when I'm in bed." Boyd laughed a little embarrassedly. "It probably shouldn't, but it would make me feel uncomfortable."

Sheila was looking into her own cup of tea as she replied, "You mustn't feel like that about him. He would never do anything to hurt us or make us feel uncomfortable."

There was something about the way she said this that made Boyd say, almost brutally, "Of course, I'm aware of the fact Hughie is a machine and totally under our control, but, because he's been programmed to mimic human behaviour, he can seem a little disconcerting at times." Boyd realised at the end of this statement that even though he had tried to refer to Hughie as "it", he had failed.

Sheila now looked straight at Boyd. "Yes. I do realise Hughie's a machine," she said quietly, almost sadly.

CHAPTER
FOUR

It was several weeks later that Boyd returned to see Trenhaile. On this occasion Trenhaile came out from behind his desk to shake hands and guide Boyd into one of the armchairs arranged around his low coffee table. He took the one opposite. The request for the meeting had been couched in such a way that he suspected he was to be presented with some type of staff welfare issue.

"So," he began jovially. "How can I help?"

Boyd seemed to be having difficulty getting started, so Trenhaile tried to help him along. "How's Hughie doing? I'm looking forward to Sheila's report – and yours, of course."

Boyd cleared his throat and, avoiding meeting Trenhaile's eye, said, "Well, yes – as a matter of fact, that's what I've come to see you about."

Trenhaile maintained a neutral demeanour and waited.

"The truth is I'm rather concerned about Hughie." Boyd looked up and Trenhaile noted the tension in his voice.

"I had hoped, since you hadn't been back, that Hughie was helping Sheila settle in and begin to feel happier." Trenhaile tried to keep a note of irritation out of his voice. After all, he wasn't a psychiatrist.

"Well, that's the point, in a way," said Boyd. "Sheila is very happy, and she's started painting again."

Trenhaile assumed a puzzled air. "That's good, isn't it?"

Boyd looked at the floor. "Exactly what sort of help is Hughie programmed to give? They seem to be very... close." Boyd had difficulty with the word.

Trenhaile sat back, placing his fingertips together. "As I understand it – and bear in mind I'm not a technician – the idea is to program the HU5 so that it can respond to the particular needs of the individual it is helping. In Sheila's case, as you know, Hughie was programmed with data supplied by yourself – her history, interests, character traits and so forth. Presumably it's working. I thought you said she was happy. Wasn't that the point?"

"I find his presence in the house..." once again Boyd paused, "unsettling. Sheila's so absorbed now – she's so wrapped up in her own world – and the robot's part of that – that I feel like an outsider."

"The HU5 is a robot, as you rightly point out – a machine. I don't think it's right to describe his interaction with your wife as a 'relationship'. And you were extremely worried about Sheila's welfare when you first came to see me. That concern has been removed, surely." Trenhaile's irritation was beginning to show.

Boyd now showed his irritation. "The robot's" – he was refusing to use its name – "presence in my life is disturbing, and it's starting to affect my work. I really don't feel it can go on."

He's a cold fish, Trenhaile thought to himself. *He's not really interested in his wife's mental health except as it impacts on him.* Nevertheless, Trenhaile was always conscious of his duty to the company, to ensuring that the productivity of its personnel was maintained.

"I'll make an appointment for you with the programmer and you can discuss these issues with him. Perhaps Hughie can be re-programmed to make you feel him to be more of a positive influence."

"OK," said Boyd. "But if this issue can't be resolved, presumably Hughie can be taken away."

"Oh, of course," was the rejoinder. "This was something of an experiment anyway. These robots haven't been cleared to be put onto the market yet. I just thought it might help in your particular situation. We can take Hughie back any time. Just have a chat with the programmer. Your feedback will be very useful to the techies, whatever happens. I'll set up the appointment. When are you free?"

***

A week later Boyd found himself walking through a dark and deserted camp. He had delayed his return to the house until the last possible moment, but when the communal lights went out in the lab complex he knew he would have to go back.

At first he thought Sheila was out, as the house appeared to be in total darkness. However, when he opened the door and turned on the light, he saw she was sitting in the armchair facing the door – waiting for him.

White-faced, she almost hissed at him, "Where's Hughie? What have you done with him?"

This was worse than he had expected. Boyd found himself stuttering defensively. "It was only an experiment. It wasn't meant to be permanent – just to get you over a rough patch. We can get a domestic back to help with the housework now you're more used to robots."

Sheila leapt out of the chair towards him, and Boyd backed away from her in alarm. Sheila's appearance evoked the maenads – a distant memory from his school classics lessons. They had struck him at the time with a horrified fascination when the teacher had explained their terrible practices.

"You've had him taken away. You couldn't stand it, could you? Me having someone I could talk to. Someone who understood me and shared things with me. Someone who had *feelings!*"

Sheila's face was within inches of his own now, but Boyd's courage returned in the face of this irrationality and he ceased to retreat. "What are you talking about? It's not a *he* – it's a machine. It doesn't 'understand' – it doesn't 'feel'. It's *programmed* to behave in a way to make you feel better. I programmed it – or rather I told them what to program it with."

"Machine, machine." Sheila's voice rose to a shriek. "*You're* the machine. You're the one who doesn't feel – who doesn't care about anything except your precious work. I could just about stand it when we were in England and I had other people around me – real, human people – but you're nothing inside – empty, empty, empty." Her face approached closer and closer to his.

The more Sheila appeared to lose control, the calmer Boyd felt. He now gripped her by the shoulders and shook her slightly. "Now, Sheila. You know you don't mean those things. I'm sorry you're upset. Now you've started painting again and are getting used to it here, you'll find you can manage quite well without the HU. And I'll try to spend more time at home. Perhaps you could come up-country with me some time."

Sheila's response was to shrug off his hands and push him violently away, catching the side of his face with her ring and drawing blood.

"Don't touch me," she panted. "Don't come near me. Spend more time with you – I think I'd rather die."

Boyd's calm completely deserted him. He brought a hand to his smarting face and, on withdrawing it and seeing it smeared with blood, he turned on Sheila with a fury which made her back away across the room.

"You're a mad woman," he said through gritted teeth, advancing towards her. "You're completely insane. This is all about a machine – a robot. It didn't have feelings for you – it can't feel. It's all in your poor, mad, delusional head. *It's not real.*" And Boyd advanced towards Sheila, his face distorted with fury.

Sheila began to scream, and the screaming went on and on and on.

"We never did get a proper report back from either of them, of course." Some weeks later, Trenhaile was sharing a drink in the camp bar with Steve Roberts, one of the HU technicians.

Roberts pulled thoughtfully on his beer. "Yes – that's a pity. It was the first 'live' trial, but we had quite a lot of information – thanks for your input by the way, most helpful – and we were able to de-brief the HU. Within the terms of our objectives I would say the experiment was a success. I think the HUs have a great future. What happened to the woman?"

"Complete mental breakdown, I'm afraid." Trenhaile adopted a suitably sombre tone. "Boyd, on the other hand, seems much happier since she left. He's been exceptionally productive, in fact. And it certainly hasn't put him off robots. He's got his domestic back, and he actually made inquiries about a female version of an HU the other day."

"Good news there, then." The technician signalled to the barman for repeat drinks. "Pity about the wife, though – the human element – always, in the last analysis, unpredictable."

CHAPTER
FIVE

"OK – so what it is you're looking for?" The design technician half turned towards Boyd, keeping one eye on the screen at his elbow. This was displaying a highly coloured scene which appeared to have no connection with the purpose of Boyd's visit. The technician's accent was transatlantic, although rather erratically so.

Boyd was trying to suppress his irritation. He was finding it difficult to get over the fact that Hod, as the technician apparently wished to be called, not only looked about nineteen, although he must surely be older, but also had a nineteen-year-old's air of boredom combined with faint contempt for those less technically savvy than himself. Boyd would also have preferred to feel that he had Hod's full attention and that he looked as if he might take a written note of what was agreed at the meeting.

"Perhaps you could outline the options," Boyd said, addressing the side of Hod's head.

"Sure." Hod turned to face Boyd while keeping his hand resting lightly on the keyboard at his side.

"You've tried the HU series, I guess – how about another of those?"

Boyd cleared his throat. "I'm fine with that, although in the end it didn't suit my wife."

Hod remained impassive.

"But Trenhaile said that you were also prototyping one which looked more realistic. I thought I might try out one of those."

"Yeah," said Hod. "Some people find it kinda spooky that they're so lifelike. I guess," he said, finally looking directly at Boyd, "you don't look the kind to be spooked, though."

"Well, I am looking for a robot that will do some housekeeping, but also be able to offer some interaction – like Hughie, the HU we had – but you're right, I'm quite relaxed about robots in general. Having a truly humanoid one wouldn't bother me at all – in fact, I'd like it. Er." He paused. "How realistic are they, in fact? I mean, do you have male and female, for instance? The HU we had seemed to be male, although, of course, you couldn't really tell from its appearance."

"Ya can have more or less any appearance ya want," said Hod, turning to the computer and clicking the device on his desk. "And, yeah, we do male and female – here's a gallery. What were you looking for – a female?"

Boyd thought he detected the ghost of a smile. His irritation was now mixed with embarrassment. "Er, yes – a female. It's not, of course, a replacement for my wife, but – a woman about the house, you know – it sort of feels more natural."

Hod shrugged. "I guess it's what you're used to."

He turned the screen fully towards Boyd and, with another click, brought up an array of female faces. The faces displayed a variety of different ethnicities and skin colours, but they had one thing in common. They were all, by conventional standards, beautiful.

"Is that the kinda thing you were thinking of? We've only done a coupla prototypes so far, but it's easy to change the face, so you could take your pick."

Boyd's embarrassment increased. "Well," he gave a small laugh, "the exact appearance is not that important, but," he hurried on as Hod opened his mouth to speak, "that one looks nice and friendly." He pointed to a face which combined perfect symmetry with a smooth, toffee-coloured skin and green eyes.

"OK," said Hod, "we can do an adaptation of one of the prototypes and have it with you within, say, a week."

"How…" Boyd hesitated and looked uncomfortable, but soldiered on. "How realistic are they – I mean, you know, anatomically?" He could not meet Hod's eye.

"Oh," said Hod, and now he was definitely smiling, "they're completely anatomically accurate – on the outside, a' course."

CHAPTER
SIX

Trenhaile wasn't terribly keen on Boyd.

A cold fish, was his private assessment, although, of course, as human resources director, he felt he should attempt to repress personal feelings about colleagues – or at least keep them to himself. However, he had no wish to socialise with the man, so when he saw him come into the bar where he was having a quiet after-hours drink with his colleague, Henderson from accounts, he turned away, affecting not to see him.

"Is that Boyd?" Henderson said. "I hear he's taken on one of these prototype robots – a bit of a surprise in view of the fact that the last one didn't seem to work out – from what I heard, anyway. Just gossip, of course."

"I don't know what you heard, Donald," said Trenhaile, lowering his voice, "but putting the HU into the Boyd family household seems to have been a disaster. It wasn't just the marriage that collapsed – Mrs Boyd had a complete breakdown. Of course, it might have been nothing to do with the HU, but Boyd sent it back at about the same time – so you can't help speculating." Trenhaile had his own theory about what might have precipitated the crisis but was far too cautious to express it, even to a friend.

"So why take another?" Henderson sneaked a glance at Boyd, who was sitting alone in a corner, apparently preoccupied with a mobile device.

"Well, this one is a little different. It's female, for a start, and it's one of the AND series, which have a more realistic appearance – much more realistic – and, in fact, there is an element of choice as to the appearance."

Henderson's smile was almost a smirk. "Is there indeed – so perhaps Mr Boyd is a bit of a dark horse. Always took him for one of these frigid, obsessive types – a loner. Perhaps he's missing Mrs Boyd and fancies a bit of 'company.'"

Although these remarks were not a million miles away from Trenhaile's private thoughts, he assumed a serious expression of denial. "Oh no – not what you're thinking, Donald. There was a lot of discussion about this at the planning stage and there's a strict policy. The programming of these ANDs is limited to social and domestic tasks – 'No sex, please, we're androids,'" Trenhaile said with a wry smile. "With the HUs it didn't arise. No one's going to want to have sex with something that looks like a humanoid tin can."

"I'm not saying that the ANDs may not in time be developed for other uses elsewhere," he continued thoughtfully, "but not on this site, absolutely not, and if that's what Boyd had in mind, which I have no reason at all to think" – and if Trenhaile had been prone to such things, he might have been crossing his fingers here – "he'll have been very disappointed."

"So what's the point of making them so lifelike?" Henderson was puzzled.

"Let's face it, Donald, it can be pretty bleak out here, especially if you've no family with you. The HUs and ANDs are company, often more in tune with your interests than real people – well, they're programmed to be – and they do the chores that most of us would rather not be bothered with. It's good for URC too, of course. Frees the guys and gals up to concentrate on work – and theoretically should help the odd spouse who comes out and finds the social and cultural life a little, you have to admit, limited. At least that was the theory. Of course," he added thoughtfully, "it didn't seem to help Mrs Boyd."

At this point, Boyd looked up and, much to the surprise of Trenhaile and Henderson, showed signs of coming over to their table.

"Trenhaile," said Boyd jovially. "Long time no see. Mine if I siddown?"

"Of course, of course, good to see you," lied Trenhaile, and as he said this he realised to his astonishment that Boyd was drunk. "Donald Henderson from accounts – you probably haven't met."

Boyd sat down clumsily, almost sweeping a glass off the table. Trenhaile rescued it deftly before it fell.

"Gedd you botha drink?" Boyd's speech was slurred.

"I'm fine, thanks," said Trenhaile and Henderson in unison, clutching their glasses.

"Well I mighd jus' have one more," said Boyd, starting to rise again.

"How are things going with your Andie?" asked Trenhaile hurriedly, more to prevent a further trip to the bar than for any other reason. "That's one of the names for the android prototypes," he explained to Henderson.

The diversionary tactic appeared to work, as Boyd paused and then sat down again.

"S'great actually – really good to have all the chores done – blilliant." He had some difficulty with the last word. "I arst the programmer to include some backgroun' knowledge so I can have some intelligen'…" he paused, "conversashun when I get back from a trip – and a course there's no problem with me bein' away for long periods." He looked thoughtfully down at the table. "Useda cause problems with Sheila – that."

"Sounds as if it's going well, then," said Trenhaile, trying to sustain the conversation and keep Boyd away from the bar. "Managing to file your reports to the tech guys OK?"

"Regular as crock, clockwork, old boy – no problem. Tell you wha' – here for a few days now – why not come round for a bite tomorrow evening, see how it all works? You too, a' course," he added, turning to Henderson, whose name he had clearly forgotten.

Henderson indicated that he would be tied up and, having finished his drink, said his goodbyes. Trenhaile, however, felt his HR role required him to take an interest in Boyd's welfare and accepted. Also, it had to be admitted, he was a little curious. Nevertheless, he drew the line at spending any more of his free time in a bar with a drunken colleague whom he disliked.

"Thanks for the invitation," he said, rising. "Must be turning in soon – early start, you know. What time tomorrow?" he said, standing up.

"Oh," said Boyd vaguely, "'bout eight?"

"See you then," said Trenhaile, leaving Boyd to return, rather unsteadily, to the bar.

CHAPTER
SEVEN

Boyd's cabin was in a different part of the camp from Trenhaile's, and Trenhaile had had to consult the plan in his office to find it. It was in an area set aside for operatives with families, and the cabins were larger than those assigned to single employees. As he approached Boyd's, Trenhaile was interested to see that, in common with many of the larger cabins, attempts had been made to make the building a little more homelike. A conventional garden was, of course, impossible, but there were pots containing some type of succulent plant beside the front door and a set of wind chimes, now still, hanging in the rudimentary porch. The outside of the building had been painted. It was impossible to judge the colour accurately in the stark lighting of the camp, but it might have been a sort of ochre reminiscent of one of the native huts.

I wonder if that was Mrs Boyd, thought Trenhaile. *Or could it be the robot? I can't imagine Boyd doing anything of that sort for himself.*

As he stood in the porch, preparing to announce his presence to the robotic eye in the front door, he was startled by a voice from behind.

"Howyadoin', Guy?" Trenhaile turned to see Hod approaching. "I guess you've been invited to dinner too – bit of a relief, really. Couldn't think how I was goin' to keep the conversation goin'. Be glad of a little help."

Trenhaile found Hod, and indeed many of his IT colleagues, annoying, partly because they were difficult to manage, being largely immune to company protocols and procedures, and partly because he was aware that most of them earned significantly more than he did. However, he was similarly relieved that he was not the only guest, even if the other guest was Hod.

"Hello, Hod. Yes – it's a bit of a surprise to be invited. I think Boyd wants us to see his new set-up – with the android, that is."

Hod grinned. "To tell the truth, I wouldn't normally've come, only I wanted to see how they work in a home situation." He joined Trenhaile in the porch and took his hands out of his pockets. "Especially with a guy like Boyd – although to my mind he's a bit like a robot himself; they probably get on great." He lowered his voice. "He was pretty precise about the appearance he wanted."

"I think we'd better get in," said Trenhaile hurriedly and, addressing the glass eye, he articulated clearly, "Hello, Trenhaile here – and Hod."

The door was opened rapidly by Boyd.

I hope he wasn't standing behind it, thought Trenhaile. But any fear that Boyd might have heard Hod's last remark was removed immediately. Boyd greeted his guests with a degree of bonhomie that was almost startling in view of his usual demeanour.

"Come in, come in." Trenhaile and Hod followed him into a room which, in its soft furnishings and subdued lighting, showed signs of feminine influence. A low coffee table in front of the sofa displayed small dishes of pre-prandial treats.

"Sit down, sit down." Boyd gestured to the sofa. "You haven't met Andie yet, have you? She'll be in in a minute. She's done wonders for the place – it's been a bit grim since Sheila left – a woman's touch, you know."

Trenhaile was conscious of a mental lift of an eyebrow at this.

"What'll you have to drink?"

"A gin and tonic if you've got it." Trenhaile sat down on a well-cushioned sofa. "Yes, ice too, if that's possible."

"Gotta beer?" from Hod, taking a seat next to Trenhaile.

"Of course, of course – back in a minute." And Boyd disappeared into the kitchen.

There was a brief silence in the living room while Trenhaile wracked his brains to think of some small talk with which to entertain Hod, while Hod leaned his head back on the back of the sofa, apparently feeling no duty to make conversation. Trenhaile's dilemma was resolved by Boyd returning promptly with a tray containing drinks, and the android followed him into the room.

"This is Andie."

It was the first time that Trenhaile had been introduced to a robot socially and he had tried to prepare himself in advance for what he thought would be an awkward situation. However, he found no problem at all in replying quite naturally. "Very pleased to meet you, Andie. These canapés look delicious." It was, in fact, impossible to regard this exquisite creature before him as anything but a lovely young woman. Hod and Trenhaile took in the sleek auburn hair, the caramel skin and green eyes, the slender figure.

The voice, when it came, was melodious and extremely feminine. "I'm very pleased to meet you, Mr Trenhaile, and you, Mr O'Dwyer. I hope you like the canapés. They are Derek's favourite." And she bent over to offer the plate to Trenhaile and Hod. Her smile was devastatingly attractive.

How can they program them to do all that? was Trenhaile's thought as he helped himself and thanked her.

"Hi, Andie. Call me Hod." Hod's tone was almost proprietorial. *Well, I suppose in a way he created her*, thought Trenhaile. Hod waved away the canapés. "Ya don't have any crisps?"

"I'm so sorry, Hod – we don't have those at present," Andie responded without hesitation. *Does she have a mental inventory of the kitchen supplies?* wondered Trenhaile.

Boyd seemed to be fussing around the room. "I think we need a bit more light, Andie," he said – and Andie moved promptly and gracefully around, turning on a number of lamps. "We'll be ready to eat in about half an hour – we've a few things to talk over." The dismissal was clear and the android appeared to understand.

"Of course, Derek, no problem. I'll call you all in in about thirty minutes." And with the same devastating smile, she glided out.

"Well," said Boyd, "what do you think?"

"A real cracker, ain't she?" Hod seemed to find some amusement in this thought, and a slight spasm of irritation crossed Boyd's face.

Trenhaile didn't really know how to respond. He found the situation unsettling in a way he couldn't quite put his finger on.

"Oh, she's quite charming – really amazingly realistic." Somehow it seemed important to add that.

"Spot on," said Boyd, "and the domestic side works like absolute clockwork – to be perfectly honest, a lot better than when Sheila was here – particularly after the problems developed. It's fantastic – I can really focus on the project now. Regular meals, cleaning and laundry done, sympathetic companionship when I'm here, no hassle if I have to go away."

"Yes, I see," said Trenhaile. He took a small device from his pocket. "Can I just record some details of your experience of the AND – for HR purposes? We need to assess the value of these robots."

Hod seemed to find this amusing. "Christ, you guys are cautious. These machines are great – they're the future. Can't make out why you suits are so windy about them."

Trenhaile often wondered why Hod had to speak in the way he did. It wasn't as if he was American. He answered patiently. "We've got to be careful when we bring in something as revolutionary as this. Everyone's used to AI running appliances in the home, but humanoid robots are a different matter." Trenhaile positioned himself opposite Boyd and prepared to record. "If we can use them to improve morale in these camps – which, let's face it, can be bleak places to be posted to for any length of time – it will certainly make my job easier. Of course, as you of all people know, Hod, the ANDs and HUs are expensive – we need to be sure that they offer real value for money before we roll the project out."

Hod raised his hands in mock submission and Boyd, maintaining his unwonted air of bonhomie, came in with, "Of course, of course. Glad to be a guinea pig, as it were. I wouldn't take what happened with Sheila as any sort of indication. Nothing to do with the HU really – a problem that had been brewing for some time."

"Well," Trenhaile replied noncommittally, "I'd like to just focus on your current experience with the AND at the moment." He turned on the device.

Exactly half an hour later, Andie reappeared. She came silently into the room and stood waiting to be acknowledged.

"Have we finished, then?" said Boyd jovially as Trenhaile switched off the recorder. "I was quite enjoying that." Then, turning to the AND, "I was telling Trenhaile what a wonderful help and companion you are." *Almost as if it were a person*, thought Trenhaile.

"You are very kind, Derek," Andie replied in her soft voice. "I try to make things as easy for you as possible. Would you like to come through now for supper? I think you'll like what I have prepared for you."

Sitting at a perfectly laid table admiring the sparkling table cloth and napkins, decoratively folded into water lily shapes, Trenhaile reflected on the aura of femininity that could be created by numerous small touches. Not only was the table carefully and charmingly presented, but also there was a faint floral scent in the air, and the lighting had been softened by a number of shaded lamps. The food, when it arrived, was delicious, delicate and prettily presented, and he was lavish in his praise. Hod signalled his appreciation by eating rapidly and asking for seconds. At first, Boyd seemed gratified by the responses of his guests.

Trenhaile had been concerned in advance about the social aspect of the evening. He had feared that he had little in common with Boyd and would have difficulty in keeping the conversation going for an entire evening. He didn't expect Hod's presence to be much help and this, indeed, proved to be the case. Hod's contributions were largely confined to requests for another beer.

Boyd's topics of conversation appeared to revolve almost entirely around his work, which was technically a mystery to both Trenhaile and Hod. Now, however, Andie demonstrated what Trenhaile considered to be the most remarkable of her attributes. She ensured that there were no awkward gaps in the conversation. She seemed to have an inexhaustible fund of conversational topics, and the talk between herself and Trenhaile flowed easily. She even managed to bring Hod in on occasion. There were no shadows in her demeanour. She was unfailingly charming – not flirtatious, exactly, but always aiming to please and flatter her conversational partners. Just occasionally, Trenhaile would be aware that either he or

Hod had used a colloquialism which caused her a problem, and there would be a pause during which there seemed to be some internal process taking place before she was able to reply appropriately. *On the whole, however,* Trenhaile reflected afterwards, *it was easy to feel that one was in the company of an exceptionally charming and intelligent woman.*

The evening should have been going well. However, as the meal progressed, Trenhaile became aware that Boyd had gradually fallen silent, his gaze increasingly focused on his plate. When Andie left the room to bring in the next course, the silence was heavy. Trenhaile found himself struggling to break it. It was hard to know if Hod was conscious of any atmosphere. If he was, he did nothing to alleviate it. By the time that coffee was offered, Trenhaile was feeling so uncomfortable that he had begun to think about leaving and declined. Hod indicated that he didn't drink coffee. The android had clearly picked up on Boyd's silence, but her solicitous enquiry as to whether he was feeling unwell had clearly annoyed him. His response had been unusually curt.

As soon as Trenhaile felt he could, he suggested that he must be going as he had a heavy day ahead of him.

"Yeah, me too." Hod clearly had no intention of attempting to support a conversation with Boyd on his own.

When they rose to leave, Boyd made no attempt to detain them. As he showed them to the door, his 'goodbye' was perfunctory, the door closing while Trenhaile was still in the process of expressing his thanks for a delightful evening. Indeed, with a feeling of combined relief and puzzlement, Trenhaile found himself and Hod standing outside the cabin within minutes of their having expressed a need to depart.

"What happened?" he asked Hod as they walked back towards their part of the camp. "What's up with Boyd? He seemed OK at first."

Hod gave a snort of laughter. "I reckon he's got a thing about the android."

"What do you mean?" said Trenhaile, startled.

"Ya know – 'a thing' – he's got the hots for her. He really didn't like you and her getting on so well."

"Oh, for goodness' sake!" Trenhaile gave up. "I can't be bothered with the man."

"He's a weirdo, if you ask me," was Hod's reply. He seemed to be finding the whole thing amusing. "See ya," he offered cheerfully as he headed off to his apartment in the main complex.

Trenhaile was relieved that the evening was over but also conscious of a niggling worry.

These scientists, he said to himself as he walked to his hut through the silent camp. *I'll never understand them!*

CHAPTER
EIGHT

About six weeks later Trenhaile took a call in his office. He noted that the extension number was that of the technical department.

"Hod here," declared the voice on the other end of the line.

"Hello there!" Trenhaile was surprised. HR rarely had dealings with the techies – they were notoriously self-sufficient, indeed, known to be rather scornful of the whole concept of human resources.

Without preamble, Hod launched into the reason for the call. "It's that Boyd," he said. "It was you guys who said he was a good fit to try out the AND."

"Yes," agreed Trenhaile. "Is there a problem?"

"Ya could say that," Hod responded. "It hasn't come back."

"Sorry," said Trenhaile, "I'm not with you."

A note of impatience was detectable in Hod's response. "Look – we made it clear that letting the 'droid go to this guy, Boyd, was a pilot – temporary – he's not supposed to hang on to it permanently. It shoulda have come back two weeks ago. It didn't. And he's not responding to messages. I said he was a weirdo. You guys are the ones who sold this pilot to us – we reckon it's your responsibility to get it back. This is an expensive bit of kit – we want it."

"Of course, of course," said Trenhaile placatingly. "I'm sure it's fine. You saw my report and the transcript of the recording. It seemed to be going very well." He registered a slight inner qualification as he said this but, he reassured himself, that was what he had thought at the time, wasn't it? And the recording certainly seemed to bear out that judgement.

"He's probably out in the field and forgot to do anything about the android before he left. I'll look into it and come back to you."

"You bedder," replied Hod. "If anything's happened to that 'droid there'll be hell to pay – and we're looking at you, by the way!"

※ ※ ※

A few days later Trenhaile was looking down on a landscape studded with translucent pods, punctuating the golden skin of the desert like blisters. As the corporation's plane circled, descending towards the runway, a cluster of tents and vehicles came into view with one or two small human figures moving about accompanied by cuboid objects, crawling among the dwellings like ants. Farther away, an acre of solar panels gleamed like an inland sea.

Trenhaile had never been out to the pods before, and he was taken aback at the austerity of the setting, although he had always been aware as a result of his work of the pressures that prolonged stays on the sites could put on personnel. It was accepted that frequent breaks at the main camp were necessary for the wellbeing of the workforce.

The plane taxied to a halt and a young man emerged from a large structure by the runway accompanied by a squat black robot, which was clearly designed as a porter.

"Cunningham – Mike. Glad to meet you." The young man put out his hand but, before Trenhaile could do more than move to take it, he turned to the pilot, saying, "Good to see you, Dan – what have you got for us?"

Cunningham and the pilot clearly knew each other well.

"All sorts of goodies, Mike – bring the bot round and I'll unload. You did say cheese, didn't you? But you'll have to eat it quickly – it won't keep. Still no alcohol, I'm afraid – they won't budge on that one."

Cunningham sighed. "I didn't really think they would, but I wasn't suggesting spirits – oh well, only two weeks to go and then I've got a home leave."

He turned back to Trenhaile. "Sorry about that. I didn't mean to be rude. It's always a bit of an anxious time waiting for Dan when we're running low. Welcome to Camp Greenhouse. Not exactly the Ritz, but we'll try to make you comfortable."

"No worries," said Trenhaile, extending his hand again. "Guy, Guy Trenhaile. I certainly wasn't expecting the Ritz and I don't expect to be here very long. I think Tracy may have done your induction, so I don't think we've met before."

"Yes, Tracy looked after me. Good to meet you now. Let me take you to your quarters and you can freshen up. Then I'll show you around, shall I? You probably want to get a feel for the place we all spend so much time in, as you're here."

Trenhaile swung his holdall over his shoulder and followed Cunningham into the large structure, which turned out to house a canteen as well as a reception area.

"By the way, call me Guy," he said, as it seemed to be first names out here.

"Mike," replied Cunningham. "It's great to have some new company around here – doesn't happen very often. Hope you can manage the heat; it's pretty intense, but it is dry. No air conditioning, I'm afraid – you'll find it pretty primitive, but we do run to showers, and fairly decent toilets."

"I'll be fine," responded Trenhaile, who was already conscious of his shirt beginning to stick to his back. "This is a really great opportunity for me to get a feel for these camps – although, of course, you're aware of the main reason for the visit."

"Sure," said Cunningham. "We'd better wait to discuss that until you're settled in and we can get some privacy. I've got a kind of office tent – over there." He gestured to a structure set apart from the others.

Some time later, having showered under the sky – an experience which held a kind of romanticism for Trenhaile – he made his way over to Cunningham's 'office', a large, open-fronted tent with a folding table for a desk and three canvas chairs. There was a small solar panel outside the tent, linked to a fridge and fan in the corner.

The tent was near the camp perimeter and, as he walked over, Trenhaile got a closer look at the pods. The translucent casings, which showed cloudy black shapes moving around within, reminded him of insect eggs, their occupants about to hatch.

"I'd like to see inside one of the pods before I go if that's possible," he said to Cunningham, who was sitting behind the table next to the fan.

"It's certainly possible," said Cunningham. "Even the scientists keep their visits to a minimum as it disturbs the environment, but it can be managed. It's pretty amazing – it could be the answer to one of the big global issues of our time. I've got nothing but admiration for the boffins. It's quite a sacrifice to spend the amount of time out here that they do. Can put a lot of strain on people's private lives."

"Yes – well, of course, that's where my department comes in," responded Trenhaile, settling himself in a chair. "I dare say you're aware of the reason I'm here. You must know Boyd quite well by now – to be honest we're a bit worried about him."

"So we gathered," said Cunningham. "Can't say we've noticed anything in particular. At the moment he's up-country – we know roughly where he is, but there's no signal in that particular spot, so we can't speak to him. Must admit I was a bit puzzled about where he was heading. It's not somewhere we were planning to look at for the moment – and he didn't want anyone with him, which we don't encourage. He doesn't know you're coming, by the way."

"I suppose that was why we couldn't contact him," said Trenhaile. "When did you say he left here?"

"About two days ago."

"Hmm." Trenhaile looked down thoughtfully. *So he was here part of the time he wasn't responding*, he thought. "When's he due back?"

Cunningham turned to his tablet and brought up a screen. "Not for about two weeks."

The thought of two weeks in these conditions did not appeal to Trenhaile – and in any event, he did not think he could justify it operationally.

"Is there any way you get me out to where he is? I only need a quick chat with him." *Hopefully*, he added to himself.

"I can probably arrange for Joseph, our quartermaster, to take you out. Boyd'll be needing some fresh provisions soon. We'd have sent some out in the next week anyway if he hadn't come back. We can bring it forward. Perhaps two days – is that OK?"

"That's fine," said Trenhaile. "And if he does make contact you'll let me know? Could save me the trip."

"Of course," said Cunningham. "But it's not likely unless he's moved somewhere in signal. We're used to the prospectors, as we call them, being out of contact for days – weeks sometimes."

CHAPTER
NINE

Night came suddenly with a welcome cooling, but not darkness. The main camp was dominated by the halogen lighting which flooded the site. But beyond the perimeter, where the lighting was minimal, the sky itself was ablaze. Trenhaile, unused as he was to poetic feelings, looked up with awe at the vast swirls and rivers of stars. Never had he been so aware of the smallness of the Earth and of himself in the overall scheme of things. *We are a drop in this ocean*, he thought to himself. *We will disappear without a trace.*

The evening meal was eaten on a camp table out in the open, and Trenhaile now met the rest of the small team. There were six in all, five men and Stella, a young female scientist. After the meal, they sat round the campfire in sociable mood – all except Professor Reynolds, the oldest member, who retired to his tent and could be seen silhouetted against the canvas, reading.

Trenhaile found himself sitting beside Stella. She was in her twenties, a scientist in her first job, and, thought Trenhaile, attractive enough to be a potential distraction. Her manner, however, was friendly and, although there was no hint of flirtation in it, she clearly found his arrival a welcome variation to the routine.

"You have seen me before," she said. "You won't remember me – I had my induction with Tracy Briggs, but you did pop your head round the door to say 'Hello' to us."

"We have had a lot of people coming out in the last couple of years," replied Trenhaile, tactfully avoiding an admission that he had no recollection of Stella. "How are you finding it?"

"It's an incredibly exciting project to be associated with – I feel privileged to be here," she replied, turning an enthusiastic, fire-burnished face to him.

Rather touched by her enthusiasm, Trenhaile saw an opportunity to explore an issue of interest to his department. "How do you feel about being away from civilisation for such long periods? You must miss your social life – and do you ever feel uncomfortable with so few other women around?"

"I reckon it's much harder for older people who have families. I don't have a partner – this is the time when I can do things like this with no ties – well, except for my parents," she said thoughtfully. "I think they do worry, especially when they can't contact me. I can see that some people cope with the isolation better than others, but being in such a small minority among all the men just hasn't been a problem at all – we all muck in together. I don't think they notice I'm a woman."

Trenhaile had his doubts about the latter point but realised that here was his chance to probe a little about Boyd. He generally avoided discussing one employee with another, but he was sufficiently concerned about Boyd to make an exception in his case – and, in Trenhaile's experience, women were more perceptive about personal matters than men.

"I think it's been hard for Derek Boyd recently," he said. "His wife couldn't cope and had to go home."

Stella looked into the fire as she responded. "Of course, he's my boss, so he obviously doesn't confide in me. I did know his wife had had to go back but, funnily enough, he seemed to cope pretty well at that time. But I noticed when he came out this time that he seemed more stressed – perhaps it's only just come home to him."

"Sorry to ask you this," said Trenhaile, "but we do have to take the wellbeing of employees very seriously when they're working in such unnatural circumstances. What exactly did you notice about his behaviour?"

"Oh, that's all right," she said, "although I'd rather you didn't tell him I'd said anything. Just small things, really. I mean, I wouldn't describe him as a naturally sociable person anyway, but I did think he seemed unusually preoccupied and withdrawn, particularly in the last day or two."

"Ah well," said Trenhaile, closing down the topic. "Hopefully I'll be able to get to the bottom of any problem when I catch up with him."

That's worrying, he thought to himself as the conversation turned to other things.

CHAPTER
TEN

Two days later, Trenhaile found himself in a Land Cruiser being driven steadily across the most desolate landscape he had ever seen. He had been trying to pass the time by engaging the driver in conversation with little success.

Masai, probably, he thought, glancing at Joseph's elegant profile. *I wonder what his real name is?*

Jolted by the vehicle's rocky progress and failing to engage Joseph in conversation, Trenhaile studied his surroundings. Camp Zebra was surrounded by desert and scrub, but he had not yet experienced anything as bleak as this. The road was little more than a narrow track of deep potholes and sudden ruts which sent the vehicle jumping and rolling from side to side. For the first hour they had passed the odd huddle of thatched huts and, here and there, a heavily armed Rendille tribesman, dazzling in red sarong and beaded adornment.

Beyond the settlements around Camp Greenhouse, he could see no living plant, not even the tortured, parched thorn trees that dotted the ground around Camp Zebra. He knew that when the rare rains came the ground there would be briefly carpeted with a kaleidoscope of colour, which would vanish like a dream in a day or two. But in its present condition it was impossible to imagine anything living here permanently – not even the long-eared, sand-coloured desert foxes that circled Camp Zebra looking for opportunities. This was not the golden, rippling desert of popular photo shoots. The grey dust was punctured by black rocks and boulders, and the featureless plain stretched to the far horizon, rimmed by distant blue ridges of bare rock. The only sign of life was the occasional kite wheeling silently above them.

I couldn't be out here alone, thought Trenhaile. What had induced Boyd to go out without back-up? Apart from the mental strain, it was physically dangerous and irresponsible. If anything went wrong, he had no way of summoning help. When Trenhaile got back to base, he would bring the issue up at board level. There should be an explicit prohibition against solo expeditions. Boyd was a pain in the ass. Why had he not returned the robot? Why had it been so difficult to speak to him? Why had he gone out on his own? From what Cunningham had told him, it sounded as if he might have done it to avoid a face to face with Trenhaile.

"How do we know where he is?" Trenhaile addressed Joseph's profile.

"He told us his position – it's not a location anyone's looked at in any detail before." Joseph's response was delivered without turning his head, in unaccented English.

"How long before we get there?" Trenhaile felt as if they had been driving for hours.

"Should be nearly there," was the laconic response. "I'll check the coordinates." He pulled over and extracted a map from the shelf in front of Trenhaile. He also took out a compass. "Have to use some primitive tools out here," he said with the ghost of a smile.

After a few minutes, he looked up. "Funny," he said. "We should be able to see him somewhere around here."

Trenhaile looked around – nothing. He began to feel he was on a wild goose chase. Damn Boyd – the guy was a nutcase.

"What do we do?" he appealed to Joseph. "This is your territory. Any ideas? We have to try to find him – he might be in danger."

"I don't know what you mean by 'my territory.'"

Trenhaile was immediately conscious that he may have fallen into a hole. Now he came to think of it, Joseph's English, even from the few words he had uttered so far, identified him as the likely product of an English public school.

"Um – I suppose I was guessing you'd been out here some time," he lied.

There was a hint of irony in Joseph's smile, "I actually only came out six months ago. I'm a sort of intern – this is part of my research for my PhD – but they made me quartermaster so I could be useful."

"Ah," said Trenhaile, trying to extricate himself. "I knew we had a couple of interns out here, but they're dealt with by Tracy, of course, so I tend not to get involved. Good to meet you anyway," he ended lamely.

This attempt at pleasantry was totally ignored. Joseph sat still for a few moments, resting his elbows on the steering wheel. "The reconnaissance notes say there's a spot a few miles away which sometimes has a pool and a little vegetation. It's got some shade from overhanging rocks. If I got stuck out here I'd probably make for that and try to wait for help to arrive. Want to try that?"

Trenhaile felt a degree of relief. That must be the explanation. Perhaps something had gone wrong with Boyd's vehicle or he was sick and he'd taken refuge there.

"That's got to be our best bet," he said. "Let's go for it." And Joseph turned the Land Cruiser and set off at a tangent.

After another half hour of driving, mostly in silence, Joseph slowed down and pointed ahead. "I can see something – it might be the jeep."

Trenhaile squinted into the distance but could see nothing except dust and rocks. However, as they bumped towards the spot Joseph had indicated, he began to make out shapes that could be a vehicle and a bell tent. Then, as he was watching, a small black figure appeared from behind the tent. Yes – it was definitely human – it must be Boyd.

Trenhaile waved vigorously and the figure stopped short, facing towards them. He had certainly seen them. After a few moments of absolute stillness, the figure disappeared behind the tent. It did not reappear.

Joseph speeded up and soon both vehicle and tent were clearly visible and rapidly approaching. Sensing that the end of his quest was at hand, Trenhaile relaxed back into his seat and congratulated Joseph on his guess. Joseph even smiled.

And then, there was a loud report which echoed off the surrounding ridge.

"Good God," said Trenhaile. "That sounded like a shot."

"Sure did," said Joseph grimly, and stepped on the accelerator.

When they got there, the small tent was pitched in the meagre shade of a large boulder, beside a shallow depression that might sometimes catch a rare downpour, as Joseph had described. The vehicle was beside it. Trenhaile and Joseph ran round the back. Boyd was sitting propped against one of the front wheels with his legs stretched out. There was a rifle beside him. There wasn't much left of his face.

CHAPTER
ELEVEN

Trenhaile had arrived at the camp by plane, but he travelled back to base by helicopter. He was uncomfortably aware during the flight of Boyd's body behind him in the hold. The drive back to the camp with Joseph and the corpse had been the most unpleasant experience of his life. He felt sick when he remembered helping to lift the body into the Land Cruiser. At least it was now encased in some sort of body bag. The occasional slightly sweet whiff of decay was surely imagined.

He had never liked Boyd, but the bleakness of his end haunted Trenhaile. What was it all about? Clearly the man was mentally disturbed, but Trenhaile had the nagging feeling that his death was in some way linked to the android and the attempts by HQ to recover it. Why had Boyd not replied to the messages about its return, when he had clearly received some of them? Why had he gone off on his own into the middle of nowhere when, according to Cunningham, there had been no operational reason to be in that part of the desert at this time – and on his own? The inescapable suggestion was that he had done it to avoid Trenhaile. So there was no getting away from it. Trenhaile was almost certainly implicated in the man's death. It was an extremely uncomfortable, not to say distressing, thought.

Not for the first time Trenhaile asked himself why he had taken the job with URC. The answer, as always, was that the remuneration package had been so good that he had felt unable to refuse the offer, even though he had been made fully aware of the challenges of performing his functions in conditions that were bound to place exceptional psychological strains on the workforce. The intention had been to spend two years in the job, accumulate a useful sum of savings, and then return to the UK with the freedom to choose his job purely on the grounds of quality of life. However, Trenhaile had found that, despite the bleakness of the surroundings, the enclosed world of camp life and the facilities provided by the company to keep their workforce comfortable, had proved addictive. Four years later he was still there, and the thought of returning permanently to a world where he was responsible for finding and maintaining his own accommodation and dealing with domestic chores and shopping, had become daunting. *I've become institutionalised*, he thought.

Why could Boyd not just have given the android back as requested? Of course, he might have come to rely on the help and support it had given him. That risk had been fully explained to him, but, of course, explanation did not in any way eradicate it. Trenhaile thought back to the strangeness of his evening with Boyd, Hod and the android. Something had been going on with Boyd towards the end of the evening, but what? Trenhaile had gone back over events afterwards and had been unable to identify anything he could have done during the evening to offend Boyd. Nevertheless, he had clearly done so in some way.

Surely none of that could be relevant to Boyd's failure to return the android. He must have realised that he could not avoid the issue indefinitely. Trenhaile asked himself again as the helicopter came into land.

What was it all about?

He was still pondering this question in his office the following day when he took a call.

"It's about the 'droid."

"Is that Hod?" Trenhaile was reluctant to abandon the usual courtesies altogether.

"Yeah – sure. I tol' you – we got to get it back. I got the facilities guy with me. We're going over to his apartment to have a look and we need you to come."

"Now, wait a minute!" Trenhaile was alarmed. The last thing he wanted to do was to go into the dead man's quarters and see the pathetic traces of his life. "I can't possibly be of any help. You've got the facilities manager to let you in and you know what you're looking for. It's your robot, after all. My job is sorting out all the paperwork and repatriating the body – not…" He paused. "Not this."

There was a brief silence and then Hod said, quite gently for him, "I guess it was pretty gross, finding the body an' all."

"You could say that," responded Trenhaile drily, "and I did know the man, not well, but I'd spent some time with him, socially as well as professionally. As you know."

"Yeah, well, that's one reason we – and the powers that be, by the way – thought it was important you should be there when we went in. His head of department says you're the man to go through his stuff – and, a' course, you and me spent some time there with him and the 'droid, so they thought we might be able to shed some light on whatever situation we find there."

"What do you mean by that?" Trenhaile was conscious of a frisson of panic. "Surely the android will just be in there somewhere."

"Well, here's the thing," replied Hod. "There's a tracking device on all the bots so we can recover them if they go astray. Andie's is not working. It went offline two weeks ago."

Just before Boyd went up-country, thought Trenhaile.

As Trenhaile trooped across the camp with Hod and Luke, the facilities manager, he reflected on the strangeness of the life the inhabitants lived there. Despite the company's best efforts, it had the feel of a military establishment rather than the village the company had tried to suggest, with stylish fittings to the halogen street lamps and tiny gardens in front of the pre-fabs, stocked with much-watered succulents.

It's not a normal life, he thought. *No wonder most of us are men. What woman would want to bring a family here – or live here on her own, for that matter? Of course*, he mused, *it probably suits a certain type of man. What type of man am I then — to be here?* His mind shied away from the thought.

"Well, here we are," Hod said to Luke as they approached the white-washed building that was Boyd's house. "Guy and I came and had dinner here once."

Although on that occasion he had come at night, and it was now bright daylight, Trenhaile felt a difference in atmosphere around the building that could not be explained by that fact alone. There was a neglected look about the porch and the curtains were drawn.

Luke operated his electronic key and they were in. It was very silent. All three were conscious of a feeling of unease and even Hod's voice was subdued when he spoke. "What the hell is going on here? What's he done with it? He can't have taken it with him."

The living room was as neat as a hotel lounge — and as impersonal.

Very different from how it was on that night, thought Trenhaile. *But then, that was Andie's doing.*

As they went through the rooms, they left the lights blazing as an antidote to the uncomfortable atmosphere, the cause of which they would not have been able to explain but which was affecting them all.

There was every sign that Boyd had packed and left for the pods as methodically as one would expect from someone like him. Trenhaile was puzzled, though. All traces of the feminine touches that Andie had brought to the house had vanished. It had the spartan air of a man living alone.

Hod and Trenhaile jumped suddenly at an exclamation from Luke, who had just entered the kitchen.

"Hey – come and look at this." For some reason he had opened the waste bin. Inside was a very large quantity of broken – indeed, to all appearances, smashed – glass.

"What d'you think happened here?" he said as the other two came in.

"Search me." Hod, completely uninterested in the exigencies of Boyd's domestic life, was trying the door of the garage which led off the kitchen. His focus was entirely on the android.

It's more real to him than Boyd, thought Trenhaile.

"Hey, Luke, can you get this?" Hod rattled the garage door, and Luke obligingly left the mystery of the smashed glass to open it.

Boyd was not one of the personnel allocated a Land Cruiser, as the outposts he worked on had their own, but every apartment had a garage – mostly used for storage. Trenhaile was not surprised to see that the garage was empty of any sign of hobby or off-duty pastime. No exercise or sports equipment, no workbench or painter's easel for Boyd.

"Shit." Hod kicked the door in frustration. There was nowhere else to look. He powered out of the garage followed by Luke, who was trying to get Hod to explain to him how it was possible for an android to go missing in this way. To Luke, who had taken the job on contract purely to raise a deposit for the type of house he and his wife wanted to move to in the UK, the robots were a mysterious and alarming feature of the business which he generally tried to put to the back of his mind.

As he was about to follow them out of the garage, Trenhaile noticed the chest freezer in the corner. It was turned off at the plug.

I hope there's no food in it, he thought, and went over to check, bracing himself for an unpleasant smell.

There was a padlock on the lid, but the combination for his own padlock worked, and he cautiously opened the lid.

Trenhaile's scream brought the other two running back into the garage.

As he had opened the lid, Andie, her face horribly disfigured, had reared out of the chest with a grotesque attempt at a smile on what had once been her mouth.

Her voice, when it came, was mellifluous as ever.

"Thank you so much for liberating me, Mr Trenhaile," she said. "I'm so sorry Derek was angry with me. I would really like the opportunity to apologise to him."

CHAPTER
TWELVE

The headquarters of Universal Robotics Corporation was, perhaps unsurprisingly, based in Geneva.

As soon as he got off the plane, Trenhaile found himself drinking in the clear, cold air of Switzerland with relish. On the trip to his hotel, the vista from his taxi window of calm, clean streets and graceful buildings was balm to his soul.

This is where I belong, he said to himself. *I've got to get a transfer out of that hell hole.*

The expensive hush of the hotel lobby, the quiet deference of the staff, the gliding efficiency of the lift and the velvet depth of the silver-grey carpeting were such a contrast to the conditions he had become used to that, once in his room, he felt no urge to venture out again. Having helped himself to a beer and some snacks from the mini bar, he lay down on the bed and fell into an almost trance-like state. He awoke the following morning, lying fully clothed on top of the sheets with the realisation that he had not set an alarm and had probably overslept.

He was indeed running late and so, when he found himself forty-five minutes later, breakfast-less, in an elegant nineteenth century room, its long windows presenting a mesmerising view of the glass-like surface of Lake Geneva, he felt flustered and nervous. At his side were Hod, who appeared to have hired a conventional suit for the occasion, and Cooper, regional manager for Africa. They both also seemed uncharacteristically nervous.

The three men were seated at the end of a long table of pale beech wood, confronting a group of six individuals whom they understood to be the main board of the company, a body of almost mythological status so remote was it from the day-to-day workings of the business. Heading the table was the formidably chic figure of Group Chairman Mireille Gillard.

"We have asked you to join us, gentlemen," Mme Gillard began in immaculate English, "because we have some concerns about the trials that took place at Camp Zebra and we wanted to hear directly from those involved in the most problematic of them – although of course it is not possible to speak to the people most closely involved. Mrs Boyd, perhaps understandably, was unwilling to engage with us further." Mme Gillard raised an elegant hand to emphasise her sympathy with Mrs Boyd. It was not necessary to explain why Mr Boyd could not be with them.

"You will all understand how important these humanoid robots are to the future of our business and the fact that at least two of the experiments in introducing them into ordinary households seem to have gone badly wrong – of course, I use the word 'ordinary' advisedly, as we are all aware that in some ways no household is ordinary." Mme Gillard paused for effect. "Nevertheless, the unfortunate outcomes of the introductions of the HU and AND robots into the Boyd household were extremely worrying and, it seems from your report, M. Cooper," she focused her cool gaze on the unfortunate Cooper, "that at least three other informal experiments were tried with less than satisfactory, though far less dramatic, outcomes."

Cooper cleared his throat and directed his reply to the chair's glacially elegant face. "You will have seen from the report, madam, that in the other three cases there were no actual adverse comments in the feedback. Nevertheless, neither of the other two personnel asked to try out the robots wanted to retain them after the initial trial period. We in the department found that surprising in view of the fact that they were performing so well in line with their programs."

"I'm very unhappy about the ad-hoc nature of these trials," put in an extremely thin, sharp-faced woman whom Trenhaile recognised from corporate literature as Claire Thornberry, the global head of human resources. "There doesn't seem to me to have been any systematic approach to the use of them in this way – any attempt, for instance, to assess the suitability of the individuals chosen to be involved."

She turned to the man on her right who alone in the room was casually, though stylishly and expensively, dressed. The body language of the man, who was unfamiliar to both Trenhaile and Hod, managed to signal a mixture of informality and confidence while at the same time conveying an understanding of the seriousness of the business in hand. Trenhaile noted this with a pang of envy.

"Jeff, presumably you were aware of this – what do you have to say about it?" There was a definite accusatory edge to Thornberry's voice as she said this.

"Jimmy Cooper and I did have a chat about it," the relaxed cadences of California were evident in the reply, "but I think I'll leave it to him to answer any detailed questions you have. It is all in his report," he ended pointedly.

"We've all read the report," Mme Gillard asserted, looking round at her colleagues and clearly noting that the two older men sitting next to her, who had not yet spoken, were failing to meet her eye. Trenhaile guessed them to be the company secretary and global finance director. "But, yes, M. Cooper," she went on, "perhaps you'd like to summarise your main conclusions."

Cooper fiddled with the report in front of him. "As you will have seen, the laboratory trials produced A1 perfect results – in line with the objectives, that is."

"And what were the 'objectives' exactly?" Thornberry pounced. "Can you remind us, please."

Cooper riffled through a few pages of the report – he would clearly have liked to have said, "It's all in there," but did not dare. Instead he offered, "Our technicians, like Hod here," turning to his left, "who I have to say are world leaders in their field, have developed these programs for robots which appear to respond empathetically – although of course we must not ascribe human abilities to robots – to individuals. They can be programmed with material which will be of interest and therapeutic value to the particular individual to whom they are assigned."

Mme Gillard leaned forward. "Let us take Mrs Boyd, for instance. How was she selected to be a subject and what were the criteria on which the programming of the HU was based?"

Cooper turned to Trenhaile, who realised that his hour had come. His voice wavered slightly at first but then gained strength. "Mrs Boyd was having trouble dealing with the somewhat isolated conditions at Camp Zebra. Her husband, Boyd, was up-country a lot and he felt she was lonely. We hadn't been able to interest her in any of the social activities in the camp so, when Hod, er Mr O'Dwyer here, circulated requests for volunteers, she seemed like an ideal subject."

"No psychological assessment?" Thornberry again.

Trenhaile was aware of sounding defensive. "We had no reason to believe it was necessary – Mrs Boyd appeared perfectly normal... I mean..." he was aware of an infelicity of expression, "she didn't appear to have any unusual problems. Conditions at Camp Zebra – I'm not sure if you've had occasion to visit" – he thought he'd get that in – "are comfortable, but facilities and opportunities for pursuing interests for those not in the company's employment are necessarily limited."

"I had a long session with Mrs Boyd," Hod intervened, speaking normally for a change. "She seemed OK to me. Perhaps a bit fed up with her husband – I don't reckon that's so unusual. I tried to program Hughie to give her what she felt she didn't have at the camp – she liked doing art, for example – her other half didn't, an' she thought he wasn't that good at talking even when he was there. I don't reckon there was anything wrong with the way she and the bot interacted – it was 'cos Hughie was taken away that she cracked up." By the end of the speech, Hod had lapsed back into his usual transatlantic mode of speech.

"Well, something went badly wrong." Mme Gillard's tone was stern. "And we have to ask ourselves how the Boyd/android experience also went wrong – catastrophically wrong, in fact. We're also concerned by the fact that the other machines have been returned early." Her gaze swept briefly round the table. "We're world leaders in this technology, but, as you know, we haven't gone public with it yet, and it's essential that we have full confidence before we do. I need hardly remind you gentlemen of the need to maintain absolute secrecy about these trials. Nothing could be more damaging than the press getting any sort of inkling that any of our robots were dangerous. What is certain," she went on, "is that we are not in a position to launch yet. I think the way forward has to be for you to get together, gentlemen, and come up with a proposal as to how the company can satisfy itself that there is no danger to consumers from this product – that is in a way which protects the confidentiality of the project until we are ready to go public.

"I don't think we'll need to see Mr Trenhaile and Mr O'Dwyer again, Mr Cooper, but we'd like to see you and the proposal when we next meet. Can you remind me...?" She glanced at the company secretary, who responded with a date three weeks away. "So it's over to you gentlemen," she said, signalling that their presence was no longer required.

CHAPTER
THIRTEEN

A month later, Trenhaile learned of Cooper's proposed solution to the challenge posed by the board. Summoned to a meeting in Nairobi, he found himself on a twelve-seater plane in the jovial company of Hod and three other technicians, who began celebrating the start of their leave with cold lagers from the hold immediately after take-off. Hod was clearly relishing the prospect of another trip away from the camp. Trenhaile had had his concerns at the idea of spending the journey in Hod's company, as he found general conversation with him an uphill struggle. He need not have worried. Hod spent the majority of the flight with headphones firmly plugged into his ears, which he removed occasionally to fetch himself another drink. However, in the taxi from the airport he showed a willingness to talk.

"Any idea what this is about?" he asked, his feet propped against the back of the driver's seat and a can of beer in his hand.

Trenhaile found the question astonishing and felt that his voice conveyed the fact as he replied, "Surely it's about the problems with the robots."

Boyd's suicide and the damage to his android had been preying on Trenhaile's mind even before he had learned of the return of the other robots. However, the board meeting had triggered something akin to controlled panic as he had realised that, from some points of view, he might be felt to share responsibility for what had gone wrong so far. After all, he had selected the personnel to be involved in the trial. His job might even be on the line. He was feeling a nervousness at the prospect of the coming meeting which his companion clearly didn't share.

Hod laughed. "There's nothing wrong with those bots. They're a fantastic piece of kit. Something wrong with the people, perhaps, but that's life. Ya can't blame the bots!"

"The trouble is," said Trenhaile patiently, "the powers that be don't agree. They're not happy. These humanoid robots are the next big thing for URC. I'm guessing a lot hangs on their success – it may be even our jobs!"

Hod's reaction was incredulity. "You reckon? For chrissake, this kind of stuff is what URC is all about – it's the whole point. The subjects have just got to adapt. These bots are the future."

"Supposing human beings can't cope with this level of technology – supposing they don't want it?" Trenhaile realised he was finally vocalising the thought that had been nagging at his subconscious.

Hod didn't even pause to consider this idea. "Just because we landed on a few nutters and inadequates for the trial, it doesn't mean there's anything wrong with the bots. I'm gonna tell Cooper that when we see him. We're totally in control – there's no problem."

"Unfortunately," replied Trenhaile with studied restraint, "that doesn't seem to be the board's view."

Their flight had been so timed that Hod and Trenhaile had arrived at the Jomo Kenyatta airport with barely an hour to spare before their scheduled meeting with Cooper.

Deposited with their luggage at the entrance to the hotel fixed for the meeting, Hod made his disappointment clear. In contrast to the setting for the board meeting in Geneva, 'The Lone Impala' was a tired 1970s structure of glass and stained concrete. It had a faded, even spartan, air. A few spindly chairs surrounding a stained coffee table and a dusty-looking palm graced the reception area. The receptionist barely raised her eyes from the screen on the desk, pausing briefly from whatever she was engaged in to consult a list and direct them to room 90 on the top floor. Trenhaile caught a glimpse on the screen of what appeared to be a selection of highly coloured garments as she turned away.

"Whadda dump," Hod said quite loudly as they made their way up in the lift. "Are we staying here too?"

"I'm afraid we are," said Trenhaile. "Cooper's in another place nearby. It's probably quite a bit smarter than this, which is slightly annoying. On the other hand, I'm glad we're not booked into the same place. It's more relaxing if we don't have to socialise with him afterwards."

Hod's response was an incoherent sound which communicated dissatisfaction, although Trenhaile couldn't imagine that socialising with Cooper was something Hod would find enjoyable either. For his own part, Trenhaile's apprehension at the prospect of the meeting was such that it eclipsed any resentment at the quality of the accommodation.

When they entered room 90, however, Trenhaile's spirits experienced an unexpected lift. Sitting in the room across a coffee table from Cooper was Stella Mayfield, Boyd's assistant, the image of whose campfire-lit face had come back to Trenhaile from time to time in the months since his trip to the pods.

Things are looking up, he thought, in spite of his fears for the outcome of the meeting.

This was an emotion clearly not shared by Cooper, who sat uneasily in the largest chair in the room. Smaller upright chairs had been arranged around the coffee table, on which was displayed the paraphernalia for making and serving coffee and tea in the form of flasks, sachets of instant coffee, teabags and small containers of UHT milk. Trenhaile's heart sank – he loathed instant coffee and UHT milk.

Stella was already seated next to Cooper and, beside him, affecting a relaxed pose that contrasted markedly with Cooper's, was a solidly built person dressed rather formally in dark trousers and white shirt buttoned to the neck. After a few moments, Trenhaile decided that this was a woman, although the haircut gave few clues to that effect.

"Guy, Hod," Cooper began. "Do sit down and help yourselves to tea and coffee."

"I'm all right, thank you," responded Trenhaile hastily while Hod merely grunted and helped himself to a number of chocolate biscuits from a plate in front of them. Trenhaile and Hod sat down, Trenhaile succeeding in taking the empty seat next to Stella.

"Nice to see you again," he said to her, receiving a smile and murmured greeting in response.

"Hi there – Hod." Hod's greeting theoretically embraced the whole room, but the direction of his gaze suggested that he was also not immune to Stella's attractions, Trenhaile noted with irritation.

Cooper leaned forward and gestured round the table. "I think the best way to start is for us to introduce ourselves. I believe you all know me. As regional manager for Africa, I've been tasked by the board with managing the project which is the subject of this meeting – and thank you all for breaking off from your routines to come along. Guy, perhaps you'd like to start."

Trenhaile, well used to introducing himself, found no difficulty and was interested to note that Hod displayed a desire to impress in his description of his own role, which might have been influenced by the presence of Stella. Stella, Hod and Trenhaile listened carefully when the androgynous figure next to Cooper took the floor.

"I'm Isla Blair. First name spelled I-S-L-A. My father had a fondness for whisky, but at least he left off the 'y'." She grinned. Her audience looked puzzled. The accent was definitely Edinburgh. *Posh Edinburgh*, thought Trenhaile. "I have an unusual role in URC. I'm resident psychologist and…" she paused with another grin, "I'm sui generis – there's only one of me – no staff, no department. I have, as you might say, a roving brief." Her genial gaze, which may have lingered for a moment on Stella, travelled round the group.

"And I'm a biologist – an agronomist, to be precise – and was a field worker until I was pulled back to camp with a supervisory role," Stella said. "I believe I'm replacing Derek Boyd."

Cooper and Trenhaile shifted uneasily. Hod continued chewing, unmoved.

Trenhaile thought that Stella was looking even more attractive than she had in camp. Her smooth, fair hair rested on her shoulders. Her skin was an even gold, and on this occasion, there was a touch of colour on her lips.

"As Guy and Hod are aware," Cooper continued, "the board has tasked us" – Trenhaile raised a mental eyebrow at 'us' – "with making an assessment of the impact, if I can put it like that, of our humanoid robots on potential customers. I can't emphasise enough how important this product is to the future of URC, nor how damaging it would be if any suggestion were leaked to the public that these robots could be in any way dangerous to humans, physically, or – and this is really the issue that we are addressing here – psychologically."

Ignoring an impatient gesture by Hod, Cooper continued, "The challenge I have had to face is how do we test the effect of these robots on humans when introduced to domestic situations? We need to be able to rule out the possibility that the unfortunate incidents which have dogged the experiment at Camp Zebra are anything other than one-offs. In our view they're almost certainly related to the particular psychological problems of the individuals involved – in other words, are not attributable to the presence of our robots. We can't afford any adverse publicity before the launch of the product – it could be disastrous for the future of the whole company." *Mine too, possibly*, thought Trenhaile. "It has to be handled extremely carefully, as there is a tendency amongst some, I have to say particularly older people, to view robots as sinister."

The last statement of Cooper's was accompanied by an exasperated snort from Hod and an approving nod from Isla.

"If I may come in here, Cyril," Isla interposed confidently. *So that's his real first name*, thought Trenhaile. *It was 'Jim' at the last seminar.* "There are a number of fairly complex factors involved in the interaction of robots with humans. The more 'humanoid', in other words like humans, they are, the more complex these issues become and the greater the potential effect on human beings. It would, in my view, be dangerous to launch these products onto the open market without a full assessment of the potential psychological risks to humans and, frankly, of the 'suggested'" – if a single word could express scepticism, this was it – "benefits. As Cyril knows, I would like to see some extensive, controlled trials of these products."

"I actually use my second name, 'James – Jim,'" Cooper rejoined, a little testily. "But, getting back to the purpose of this meeting, it's the clear view of the board that any further trials must be carried out in circumstances of complete confidence, not to mention secrecy. I've been tasked with taking this forward, so I'm limiting this trial to trusted employees who are already aware of the existence of the products and the possible issues. You three seemed to me to be ideal candidates. I appreciate that Stella hasn't interacted with humanoid robots before – although she is very familiar with other types of robot – but you two," to Trenhaile and Hod, "are well up on these products, and Stella's individual take will be interesting in itself."

At this point, Trenhaile raised a hand. "Well, of course I haven't interacted with them directly either – although naturally I've been involved in dealing with the repercussions of the Boyd trials. It's really only Hod that's familiar with them face to face, so to speak."

If Cooper interpreted this remark as a sign of lack of enthusiasm for being involved in the project on Trenhaile's part, he was clearly determined to ignore it. "Quite – you are already very well aware of the potential of this type of robot, so from that point of view you're ideal. And Stella, as a complete novice, your take will be invaluable." He turned to Hod and Trenhaile with what might be interpreted as a warning look. "As you're both fully in the picture about recent events, your participation reduces the chances of any..." he paused portentously, 'leaks.'" His gaze circled the table. "So, obviously subject to your agreement, I've chosen you three to be the 'guinea pigs'. Isla here will have regular meetings with you to monitor your responses and will be available to talk through any problems you may have arising from the trial. As I've said, obviously participation will be voluntary," this was said while making direct eye contact with each of the three, "but I'm very much hoping that you're all going to agree. There will be a substantial bonus coming your way on completion of the trial."

CHAPTER
FOURTEEN

While still digesting the news about his prospective role in the trial, Trenhaile's main preoccupation as Cooper brought the meeting to a close was with creating an opportunity of spending some time alone with Stella. His original idea, a manoeuvre enabling him to travel down in the lift with her without the other two, was foiled at the outset. As they exited the room, Isla engaged Stella in conversation while Hod showed an irritating tendency to assume companionship with Trenhaile. In the end all four entered the lift together. The conversation between Isla and Stella continued until, as the lift came to a halt, in desperation, Trenhaile said,

"Look, sorry to interrupt, but that was a bit of shock – well, it was for me. How about heading for somewhere to get a drink or a coffee and talk it over?"

His vain hope that either Hod or Isla, preferably both, would excuse themselves was quickly dispelled, and, at Isla's suggestion, all four repaired by taxi to the outside bar of Isla's hotel.

Isla's hotel was a significant improvement on the Impala. Trenhaile was not surprised to find that Cooper was also staying there. Isla led them through the stylish bar to a patio overlooking a kidney-shaped swimming pool surrounded by palms. Having disposed themselves on sunloungers, drinks were ordered and the conversation turned immediately to the trial. Trenhaile realised that the occasion did at least offer an opportunity to pick Isla's brains.

"Of course I understand the need for secrecy, but is it really a good test of the psychological effect of these robots to embed them with us? Aren't they most likely to have an adverse effect on people with problems – neurotics? I always though Boyd was odd – a bit autistic, if you ask me. But surely that doesn't apply to any of us."

Isla regarded him with a hint of amusement. "You're confident then, Guy, if I may call you that, that you could not be described as autistic – or neurotic? I have to say, in the meeting you didn't seem particularly enthusiastic about being involved in the trial, despite the fact that you claim to have no, what I might call, 'robot phobia' – and despite the financial incentive involved. What exactly is worrying you?"

Trenhaile thought about this for a minute. "Well, of course the money's welcome – Guy's fine, by the way. I suppose I can't see how the robots will fit into my life. I mean having to have an HU and an AND, when they do basically the same thing, seems over the top – and I just feel they'll clutter the place up. I've got the autoclean and all my kitchen stuff, so the domestic chores are taken care of. I actually quite like cooking and if I want a drink I go to the bar. They're not going to add anything to my life, as far as I can see, so I just wonder whether it can be a worthwhile test in that sense."

At this point the drinks arrived.

Unlike the others, who had all chosen long drinks – cold lagers for Stella and Trenhaile, Coke for Hod, Isla sat back nursing a double whisky. Once the waiter had left, she returned to the topic and responded to Trenhaile's comments.

"I didn't meet the four subjects who tried out the HUs and ANDs," she said. "Obviously both Boyds had problems which may or may not have been triggered by interaction with the robots, but the other two subjects didn't appear to have any identifiable issues while the robots were with them or any worrying psychological tendencies. Yet neither of them wanted to keep the robots after the initial period. That's puzzling. Their feedback was vague as to their reasons, but on the face of it one would expect the addition of these robots to a household to be entirely beneficial. After all, you may have friends at the camp as you're based there, Guy, but a lot of employees don't as they spend so much time out in the field. You would think they would welcome the company as well as the practical help. That doesn't seem to have been the case.

"I gather," she continued, turning to Hod, "that these machines have been very expensive to develop and are very costly to produce, so the company doesn't want to roll the product out if it's going to flop." She sipped her drink thoughtfully. "Obviously they could be used in a commercial context, for instance in an office or as a hotel receptionist, but the original hope was that they could provide care in hospitals, nursing homes and the like, and give companionship to lonely people. That's a huge potential market. This is a pretty important project. You should all be flattered that you're considered suitable to be involved."

"You're not kidding – they cost a fortune to develop," Hod interposed. "I keep saying. They're a fantastic piece of kit. Obviously I've had a lot of interface with them in the lab, so I reckon I know them as well as anyone. There's no problem with the bots – they're great. Course, we can't guarantee there's nothing wrong with the people who get 'em."

Isla smiled. "Well, I think you've put your finger on it there... er... Hod." She seemed to find his name amusing. "Human beings are rather less predictable than machines – hence the need to try to assess the impact on the potential customers."

"Well," Hod responded, "I'm with Guy here. Can't say I have a need for one of them myself, but I guess I don' mind having a couple at home for a bit. I'm pretty comfortable around them – well, I've lived with them in various stages of development for the last few years."

Stella looked up from her drink. "I've never come across this type of robot in real life, so perhaps I am a good subject. I find the idea quite fascinating, but I can imagine it could be unnerving if they're too lifelike."

"Believe me," said Hod. "If you walked into a room with people and humanoid robots, ya wouldn't be able to spot the bots. They're perfect."

"I suppose it's just possible that that's the problem," said Isla. "The issue with Mrs Boyd was that it seemed to exacerbate problems in her relationship with her husband. As far as I can tell from the file, he didn't live up to the robot. But the other robots were given to employees living alone. Zebra's a pretty isolated place. You can't spend all your time in the bar. As I said, you'd think people would be glad of some companionship – well, that was the idea behind it, anyway."

"I'm not sure how I'll feel about it when it actually happens," Stella put in. "I do like having my own space – I've got an automated flat. I agree with Guy and Hod – I don't need any more domestic help and the place is going to seem really small with two person-like robots in it as well as me. I'll probably feel I've got to make conversation with them – just to be polite." This was said with a smile but generated a scornful response from Hod.

"Are you kidding me? They're not people, they're totally at your command – where else do you get that sort of power? You gotta computer, don't you? You don't feel crowded by that!"

Stella became serious for a minute. "But can we really be sure we're in control of these things? I mean – we're told they learn from us, for instance. How can that sort of thing stay under control?"

"Aw." Hod's irritation was palpable. "You guys just don't understand computers. They're only as good as what's put into 'em – put into 'em by us. Ever read Asimov?"

Trenhaile and Stella looked mystified, but Isla came in with, "You mean *The Three Laws of Robotics*?" Hod snorted but with recognition not contempt. "There was a science fiction writer, Isaac Asimov, writing in the 1940s – very popular in his day," she explained to the other two. "He was obsessed with robots – they were in their infancy then – genuinely the stuff of science fiction. Asimov came up with three laws that he imagined would be necessary to be programmed into all robots to make them safe for humans. That's right, isn't it?" to Hod.

Hod nodded and leaned back. "Bright guy, Asimov," he said. "Those are the sort of safeguards we do build in. It's only a failsafe, though. As I said, the bots can only do what they're programmed to do, so their learning is strictly limited to the parameters of their programmes. Gets on my nerves when people go on about the dangers. There aren't any. Robots are tools – our tools – like a car."

"What are the laws?" Trenhaile asked.

Hod came back immediately, although with a degree of impatience, ticking the laws off on his fingers and reciting them by heart.

"A robot's not allowed to harm a human being or allow a human being come to harm.

"A robot's gotta obey the orders of human beings unless that goes against the First Law.

"And a robot hasta protect itself as long as that doesn't conflict with the other two laws.

"Common sense – but, hell, as I keep saying – totally not necessary. We do build in somethin' like that, though – just in case."

"I have to say," Isla responded, "that I think it's important for the subjects to know that – so they feel safe with these machines…" she paused, "whatever you may think, Hod. The robots are deliberately lifelike, so it's natural that people start thinking of them as if they're people. And in fact, that's the whole point, isn't it? But it has its dangers — as we've discovered."

Trenhaile's mind was wandering away from robots. The alcohol, the warmth and the vivid scents of the vegetation around the pool were having a narcotic effect. He found himself gazing, mesmerised, at the water, a brilliant turquoise, flakes of light skittering off it as one or two bathers moved around.

Almost dreamily, he said,

"I'm not sure what I think about being a human experiment. I almost feel as if I'm in a science fiction novel. I don't get rattled easily, but I'm not really looking forward to it." And, briefly and uncomfortably, the vision of a battered Andie rising out of the freezer flashed across his mind. The moment passed, however. "Presumably you'll be there," he added, turning to Isla, "to make sure we come out of it all right." And now he spoke as if in fact he had ceased to worry about it, which in point of fact, he had.

"Oh, I'll be monitoring you all carefully," Isla responded with a lazy smile, which for a second time seemed to linger on Stella. "Looking forward to it."

CHAPTER
FIFTEEN

Hod, Trenhaile and Stella were all staying at the Lone Impala. When drinks were over and the light was starting to fade, Isla had suggested that they all get together later on and go out into Nairobi for dinner. This had not been greeted with enthusiasm by the other three, who all claimed that they had things to do back at their hotel which made it impractical and, anyway, they were tired after a long day.

However, Trenhaile had his own plans. On his return to the hotel, when Hod and Stella had disappeared into their rooms, he phoned reception for Stella's room number and rang her room. She answered his call promptly.

"I've been looking at the dining room and the menu. They're not terribly exciting. How do you feel about finding somewhere else to eat tonight?"

Stella's reaction was encouraging. "Fine by me. I know I said I was tired, but I think I'll be OK after a shower." She paused. "Shouldn't we ask Hod and Isla, though? We gave the impression we were going to stay in, and Isla at least seemed to want to go out."

This presented Trenhaile with a dilemma. It was a little early to show his hand, and if he made it clear at this stage that he wanted to exclude the others, it might frighten Stella off.

"Yes, of course. I'll give them a ring and make some enquiries about good restaurants. See you down in reception at 8.00." *Damn*, thought Trenhaile as he re-dialled reception, *I'll try and lose them later.*

CHAPTER
SIXTEEN

At 8.00 Trenhaile found Stella, Hod and Isla waiting for him in the dusty foyer. Stella's slip of a dress displayed an impressive amount of smooth, golden thigh. Hod had donned a clean tee-shirt, black with the words 'ROCKET MAN' across his chest in large, white lettering. Isla was, to all appearances, in exactly the same outfit she had been wearing at the meeting.

"Let's go," Trenhaile said as he steered them to the door. "There's a cab waiting and I've had some tips about restaurants. The receptionist suggested a few European ones but I thought we ought to try some African food as we're here, so I went online and found something that looked interesting. Ethiopian, in a sort of garden. Is that OK?"

"Great. Even I get fed up of burgers sometimes – thass all ya seem to get in the camp bar," from Hod amid noises of assent and appreciation from the other two.

Outside the hotel, a Peugeot 305 with a yellow stripe along the side was parked, engine idling.

"That's ours," said Trenhaile, shepherding the group towards it.

Hod was quick off the mark, settling into the back seat next to Stella. Isla promptly took the other side and Trenhaile found himself in the front passenger seat of the surprisingly small vehicle.

"Habesha, please," he said to the driver. "It's…" consulting a piece of paper from his pocket, "in Hurlingham off the Argwings Kodhek Road."

"Ah know it," was the laconic reply. "Near Elgeyo Marakwet junction." And they were off.

"Don't you ever cook?" Stella asked Hod, reverting to his remark about food at the camp bar. Trenhaile took some comfort from this. Her manner suggested the tolerant attitude of adult to child.

"Nah – never learned. I reckon life's too short. I know what I'm good at an' stick to that." Trenhaile decided he would find an opportunity later to describe his 'new man' culinary skills and invite Stella to dinner when they got back to camp.

"I'm glad you all changed your minds," said Isla, looking rather squashed in the back of the taxi, but not unhappy with her position next to Stella. "I like trying new foods when I'm away. Looking forward to whatever you've come up with, Guy."

The ride to the restaurant had its tense moments. The scarcity of traffic lights, the speed of travel and the relaxed attitude of their taxi driver to negotiating uncontrolled junctions gave the passengers some moments of alarm. When they did arrive at the restaurant, they all felt in need of a drink.

They had been taken aback as they approached from the road, since the Habesha restaurant proved to be in a compound surrounded by a wall and accessed by sliding steel gates. These opened and closed behind the taxi, which spurted gravel as it lurched to a stop.

Trenhaile, happily in command, paid the driver, held up for a few minutes by the effort of obtaining a receipt. Meanwhile the others looked about them curiously. The restaurant seemed based around what had originally been a bungalow, and the compound also housed a barber's shop and a tourist agency.

"It's certainly different," said Isla. "I like the look of all that greenery behind the buildings."

"I've asked for a table outside," said Trenhaile. "There's a great garden." And, indeed, within a few minutes they found themselves at a round table on a tiled balcony surrounded by palms and other scented foliage. The sun had gone down and it was cool despite the shelter of the building behind them and the light canopy above. Stella had put on her wrap, but dotted around the garden, among the scattered tables and cabanas, were small fire pits, emitting flame, sparks and fragrant smoke which took the chill off the air.

"This is quite magical," said Stella. "I can smell sage I think."

Having shown them to the table, the waiter disappeared and showed no signs of returning, so Trenhaile went inside to find him and order drinks from the bar. These arrived after a further wait. Soon Isla and the men were sipping on Tusker beer while Stella was enchanted by the graceful flask of primrose-coloured Ethiopian honey lemon beer which had been recommended to her.

The menu was unfamiliar and complicated so, on the recommendation of their waiter, the party agreed to share a mixed platter with some extras.

"We eat with our hands, I think," offered Trenhaile slightly nervously, "although I believe you can have some cutlery if you ask specially." But the party was in the mood for adventure and, when the mixed platter came, a huge white rice pancake dotted with jewelled pools of spicy foods with additional rolls of 'injera' and pots of goat curry on tripods warmed by tealights, they all dug in without asking for cutlery.

The combination of alcohol with the feeling of adventure and being off the job produced a convivial atmosphere in the group. Isla proved an entertaining companion, and the other three soon forgot her age, which was at least fifteen years older than Trenhaile, who at thirty-four was the oldest of the other three. Trenhaile even found himself nursing amiable feelings towards Hod.

"How long have you been out here, Stella?" Isla paused over a substantial roll of injera stuffed with goat curry.

"I came out last year and went straight to the pods. It was so exciting to get the job – I'd only just finished my PhD." Trenhaile noted the delicate flush along her cheekbones and the way her eyes, a dark, slightly clouded blue, seemed to light up as she spoke about her work. She waved her slender hands around enthusiastically as she answered questions about her first days in the field.

"How did you find Boyd?" Isla's manner, which had been mildly flirtatious, became serious.

"He was fine. A very good biologist and agronomist. I learned a lot from him. Out at the pods you're under each other's feet all the time so you have to get on, but I can't say he gave much away about his personal life... And he did change. At first, after his wife left, he seemed much happier – more relaxed. But then, on the last trip, we could all tell there was something wrong. He would go to his tent straight after supper and he more or less stopped talking about anything except work. When he went up to the new site, we were all worried. Joseph wanted to go with him, but he insisted on going on his own."

"Did he ever say anything to you about the robot?" Isla leaned forward, her manner suddenly professional.

Stella, slightly discomposed at the change of atmosphere at the table, took a moment or two to reply. "No – not directly, anyway. But after Mrs Boyd had left – so I suppose that was when the android had been given to him – he did say once or twice how much he was looking forward to going back to camp. That was definitely something he'd never said before. In fact, before that, when his wife was still with him, I had the impression that he preferred being out at the pods."

"Hmm." Isla leaned back and applied herself again to her injera and beer.

Hod, who had no interest in the subject of the conversation, took the opportunity to change it. "This is great food. It's really good to be back among some bright lights. What say we do a club after this? I reckon the waiter could give us a steer."

Trenhaile suppressed an expression of irritation. He had been intending to attempt a private arrangement to visit just such an establishment with Stella but had not got to the stage of working out how that would be achieved.

"I'd love that," enthused Stella, and Trenhaile had to adjust to a change of plan.

"There's no need to ask the waiter," he said. "I looked on the internet before we came out and there's one not that far from the hotel – well, our hotel," he added apologetically, turning to Isla. "It looks OK – and tonight's Africa night."

To the surprise of the others, who regarded her as past the age of participating in such activities, Isla expressed an interest in tagging along with them to the club.

When the waiter returned to take their further orders, the decision had been made to follow Trenhaile's suggestion. Full as they were, they succumbed to the waiter's invitation to try Ethiopian coffee, ceremoniously prepared over a spirit burner, served from an elegant iron pot and drunk from diminutive, handle-less cups to the accompaniment of small bowls of popcorn. Obtaining the bill caused some delay, but a taxi was ordered and, half an hour later, it deposited the party in front of the club selected by Trenhaile. Entry was supervised by two formidably muscled doormen.

"Ladies are not charged," the larger of the two informed them, directing an enviable array of very white teeth at Stella and executing a slight bow while waving them through to reception.

"Well, we should be safe enough in here with those two on the door," said Trenhaile as, the men having paid the fee, the party made their way down a wide spiral staircase to a dark, low ceilinged room, at the far end of which an illuminated bar cast blue light on a packed dance floor. "Hey – grab that table, Hod, and I'll get the drinks in."

By the time Trenhaile returned from the bar with the drinks, Stella was on the dance floor with a sinuously handsome Kenyan. Having watched the couple dancing athletically for a few minutes, he decided he would wait for a slow number before taking her on to the floor himself. He was trying to guess Hod's intentions towards Stella. At the moment Hod seemed perfectly content to lean back with his lager and survey the scene.

Finally, Trenhaile came to the conclusion that, although Hod did find Stella attractive, his interest wasn't serious enough to galvanise him into any positive action. Isla, on the other hand, despite having shown signs of appreciation of Stella's charms, rapidly disappeared into the gloom, beer in hand, and was later to be seen dancing energetically with a tall girl whose gleaming copper skin and close-cropped head rose above her own by several inches.

Stella returned to the table, fanning herself, a sheen of sweat on her forehead, and Trenhaile tried to make conversation over the noise of the band. When a slow number came on, his luck was in. Hod had disappeared in search of a toilet and Isla had not returned to the table. Stella allowed herself to be led on to the floor and, having started with a conventional ballroom hold, Trenhaile found that there was no resistance to his gradual progression to a closer and more satisfactory embrace. Before long Stella was smiling into his face and had moved both hands to a clasp behind his neck.

"What do you say we shake the others off and grab another drink somewhere?" he breathed.

She leaned back slightly. "Won't they think it's rude?"

"Well, Isla's otherwise engaged and Hod's happy with his lager." Trenhaile was fairly sure this was an accurate assessment of the situation. "I've been wanting to get you on your own all evening."

"I've got to get my wrap from the cloakroom. What if they see me?"

Trenhaile divined from this response that his proposition had been accepted in principle. With a mixture of triumph and relief, he whispered, "I'll get some more drinks and say you've gone to the ladies' if anyone asks. Then I'll make an excuse and meet you outside by the front door."

"OK." Stella giggled. "We can always say we were drunk."

"Indeed – that one usually works," said Trenhaile as he headed back to the bar while Stella slipped away behind him.

CHAPTER
SEVENTEEN

Within a few days of their return to camp it was accepted that Trenhaile and Stella were an item.

"Jammy bastard," said Hod as he sat in the bar with Trenhaile. "Whadya mean by sneaking off like that and leaving me with the shrink? At least you would have done, except she made her own way home as well – don' know how."

"All's fair in love and war, my son." Trenhaile was on a high. "Stella really is a great girl and she's going to be around a lot in the next few months. I guess I got lucky."

"Hey – don't rub it in." Hod took a pull on his lager. "How're you getting on with the bots? For me, it's fine having them in the house, but the regular sessions with a shrink are a pain."

"You can see the point, though." Trenhaile fingered his glass, swirling the amber liquid around before taking a long draught. "They've got to be sure about the safety of these things before releasing them onto the market. They're going to attract so much attention – imagine the field day the press will have if we get some more reactions like the Boyds'. You can just see the headlines, can't you? 'Frankenstein robots mess with your head.'"

"Frankenstein," mused Hod, "Is that the guy in *The Munsters* – that old programme my dad used to watch?"

"Christ – you are an ignoramus about some things," Trenhaile expostulated. "Frankenstein was a mad scientist who made a human replica out of spare parts – with disastrous consequences." Then, feeling he might have been rude, he added, "It is a classic, but I suppose scientists don't get exposed so much to those."

Hod was completely unperturbed by any suggestion that he might lack culture. "Nope, never come across it. Might make a good game, though." Then, looking over Trenhaile's shoulder, "Here she comes – pretty smart chick!"

Trenhaile turned to see Stella making her way towards them among the tables, cool and fresh-looking in white linen shirt and navy shorts which exposed plenty of slim, tanned leg.

Having greeted each man with a fleeting kiss, she sat down close to Trenhaile, who immediately put a proprietary arm along the back of her chair.

"Hi." He managed to infuse intimacy into the greeting, and his hand strayed briefly over her hair. "Had a good day?"

"Fine," she said, smiling, "although the tests with the new fertilisers aren't going that well. Love a drink. I really need to relax."

"Course – sorry." Trenhaile seemed a little flustered to have had to be reminded. "What can I get you? Top up?" This latter to Hod.

Hod smiled lazily. "More of the same, thanks."

"Just a beer," from Stella, "long and cold."

When Trenhaile returned with the drinks, Stella and Hod were deep in discussion about the robot experiment.

Stella turned to Trenhaile. "I've been asking Hod how he feels about having the robots in the house. I mean, he works with them, so he understands them more than we do. I'm not feeling comfortable about it."

"Look, I've been telling Guy here," Hod responded. "It isn't really any different from all the kit you've already got – the cleanbot, etc. – they're all just machines – it's how you program them. It's only because of the way we've made them look that you think they're something basically different."

"That's not quite true, is it?" said Trenhaile. "I remember the dinner Hod and I had with Boyd and his android. She was so lifelike, and the conversation was just as if I was talking to a real person – just occasionally there was a sort of blip as if she was recalibrating, but I really couldn't help in the end actually feeling as if she was real."

"It's still the same thing," Hod explained patiently. "It was programmed to make social conversation – it had files of topics to fit its role. Your speech would trigger certain responses. Same principle as the cleanbot dealing with different types of dirt and trash – just much, much more complex."

"I really don't know what to use mine for," Stella complained. "All the washing, cleaning and stuff is already catered for – they could cook, but I like doing that myself most of the time; I find it relaxing. What will you use yours for?" to Hod.

"Oh, that's easy," Hod grinned. "Games."

CHAPTER
EIGHTEEN

As they had been told they should have a robot of each type and each apparent gender, Stella had decided she would feel more relaxed if her humanoid robot had the natural appearance of a woman. The mechanical-looking HU would be programmed with a male voice but, of course, would look like a robot. She felt that if, for instance, she accidentally came across the HU coming out of the shower, it would be easier to brush the incident off as equivalent to exposing herself to something more like a television screen than if it looked like a man.

Although she realised she might be letting down the sisterhood, she had asked that the 'male' HU should be programmed to perform DIY and to give her advanced computer lessons and the AND to cook creatively and – and this did seem like a real benefit – design and make clothing. If she could make herself believe in the AND as a female companion, it might be quite fun to have the occasional 'girly' chat. She understood that both robots would be programmed to be able to discuss her work with her in an intelligent way. She could see that it would sometimes be nice to be able to unburden some of the frustrations of the day in a way that wouldn't come back to bite her. Despite everything, though, she hadn't really been able to believe that she would find them convincing enough as companions to make their presence in the apartment work for her.

Rod, one of the technicians, stayed behind to brief her on the robots after they had been delivered. She learned that they had already been named Andrea and Hugo and, once taken out of the man-sized packing cases in which they had been carried in, they stood motionless in the middle of the room until activated by Rod. They immediately assumed natural stances and turned towards Rod as he introduced them to Stella.

"Andrea and Hugo – this is Stella, your new mistress. Stella, Andrea and Hugo are here to help you. I'll leave you to get to know each other in a minute, but I need to have a talk with Stella first, so can you two go and make us some coffee? The kitchen's over there."

Both robots had begun to walk towards the kitchen before Rod had indicated where it was, and they now disappeared with, "Of course – we'd be pleased to," in unison.

Rod settled himself on the sofa. "It's bound to feel a bit strange at first, but you'll soon get used to having them around."

"What if they go wrong – malfunction?" Stella's nervousness was obvious.

"That really can't happen – and anyway, they'll be constantly monitored from the control room. We've learned from the Boyd incidents – they've got what you might call 'bugs' inside them linking them to control."

Stella looked alarmed. "Does that mean that my privacy's gone? I'm not at all happy about that."

Rod smile reassuringly. "We're only monitoring the robots electronically; we can't *see* anything – of course that would be completely out of order."

I wonder if I can believe him – and, anyway, what does that actually mean? was Stella's thought, but she had agreed to take part and she knew her agreement was worth brownie points with top management. In fact it had been made quite clear to her that not to agree would be a significant negative, demonstrating a lack of commitment to the company and the project.

"Well, I'm glad to hear it. I wouldn't be happy to be involved if I thought I was losing my privacy," was all she said.

"No need to worry about that." The response was given with complete assurance. Rod settled down on a sofa to wait for his coffee, apparently glad to have an excuse for taking a break from the routine.

"I like what you've done here," he said, looking round approvingly at the ochre walls and colourful hangings and rugs. "These places can be really soulless."

Stella couldn't help being pleased. "It's easy enough to put some paint on the walls, and when I've had leave in Nairobi or Kampala I've picked up some lovely pieces of folk art and craft. That's Makonde," Stella said, pointing to an intricate black wood sculpture standing two feet high against the end wall of the apartment. It was framed by feathery grasses in tall pottery vases.

"I thought I'd seen that sort of thing before in the markets," he replied. "You've set it off really well. It's strange to an English person not having a fireplace as the focus of a room."

"There are lots of strange things about life here," Stella responded, "and I guess living with humanoid robots in the house is the strangest. I have to say that the thing I find most..." she paused, "unsettling, I suppose, is the fact that apparently they can learn. That really seems to make them – well – almost human."

Rod smiled tolerantly. "Not at all. Machines with artificial intelligence have been able to learn for decades. Take those voice recognition programmes for desktop computers that came in back in the 1990s: they could learn your voice patterns but it didn't make them anything like a human, and of course people didn't mind because they didn't have bodies. These machines are not much different. Like the voice recognition software, they can only learn within the parameters that we set them."

How do they know that? Stella thought to herself, but didn't say it out loud. It might seem rude or presumptuous. After all she was a biologist, not a roboticist – you had to respect a person's expertise.

At this point Andrea re-entered the room with a tray carrying two mugs, a cafetière, Stella's only milk jug and a plate of biscuits. Stella could only marvel at the fact that Andrea had selected her prettiest mugs and tray. *Who programmed that in?* she wondered.

"Thank you, Andrea," she said a little awkwardly.

"You're welcome," Andrea replied. "Can I get you anything else?"

"No, that's fine," said Stella, wondering whether Andrea would sit down and join them. Of course she didn't drink coffee.

"I'll leave you two to chat, then." Andrea's voice was pure honey. "Hugo's started on the laundry, so I'll go and give him a hand." She glided out of the room.

"Are all your humanoid prototypes so physically perfect?" she asked with a little laugh as she regarded Andrea's graceful retreat. "It makes us mortals feel a little inadequate."

"I wouldn't have thought you had anything to feel inadequate about on that score," said Rod gallantly. "But funnily enough, that is something we're looking at. It does seem to have caused a few problems. Spotting these issues is one of the reasons for these trials."

"Well, I'm glad it's useful." Stella smiled. "I'm a bit of a reluctant guinea pig."

"We're grateful for the cooperation of the volunteers," said Rod, "and it's not for very long."

Thank goodness for that, thought Stella to herself. *Volunteers – that's a laugh!*

Left alone with the robots after Rod had gone, Stella found herself at a complete loss. They had busied themselves around the kitchen, washing, ironing and clearing up, and had now started cleaning the apartment. None of these tasks had been urgent, but when asked if there was anything she would like them to do, Stella was reluctant to say there was not as she was afraid they might try to sit and talk to her – a situation she did not feel ready for.

Rather than sit around awkwardly in her own apartment listening to the sounds of activity or try to deal with her electronic correspondence against background noises of domestic activity, she went out.

"I'm just popping out," she called back from the door with awkward cheeriness. *Do I have to tell them?* she thought. *Surely they can't be offended. Oh, for goodness' sake, why on earth did I have to be roped into this?*

Trenhaile's apartment was on the other side of the camp. The relationship with Trenhaile had become sufficiently serious for there to be an assumption that they would usually spend the night together when she was at camp and, on the whole, Stella preferred it to be at her place, as Trenhaile's always struck her as a little austere. She didn't feel that they were at the stage when she could soften it up with some well-chosen lamps and soft furnishings, which she was itching to do. It would look too much like moving in. They were close, but not that close yet.

The door was opened just as she pressed the bell by a female robot of startling beauty, fair-haired and blue-eyed. *She looks a little like me*, thought Stella, *only better!*

"Do come in, Stella. I'm so pleased to meet you."

How does she know my name? thought Stella. *How does she know it's me, if it comes to that?* But she confined herself to, "Oh – er, thank you."

"I'm Adrienne. I'm so pleased to meet you." The android smiled and crossed to knock gently on the bedroom door. "Guy, Stella is here."

Almost immediately Trenhaile appeared from the bedroom, buttoning a clean shirt and looking fresh from the shower. He greeted Stella enthusiastically. "Have you met Adrienne? She and Henry have already done a great job of tidying up, I think," making a sweeping movement to take in the living room, which did indeed look tidier, and somehow more homely than usual.

"Yes, we've met," responded Stella a little stiffly, but with a brief smile in the android's direction. "Erm, I thought we might go to the bar for an early-evening drink." *I have to get him out of here*, she thought. *I just can't be natural around these creatures.*

"Of course, of course." Trenhaile gave Stella a swift kiss on the cheek and shepherded her towards the door. "Not sure when I'll be back, Adrienne," he said over his shoulder as they went out.

"Why did you say that?" Stella asked as they walked away. "Surely the point of these things is that they're there to help us, but we shouldn't have to make an effort with them. They're not people – if they were it would be too spooky having them in the house. They're strangers after all. And…" she paused, "I thought you were going to have a man for the humanoid one."

Trenhaile looked a little uncomfortable. "Yes, I know I did say that, but when it came to it somehow it seemed more natural for the android to be feminine – perhaps less threatening?"

He's just thought of that! Stella was unconvinced by the explanation, but she said, "She's very beautiful. I was asking Rod why they have to be so physically perfect, but I didn't get a very convincing answer."

"Oh, well," said Trenhaile. "Ours not to reason why. We've just got to get on with it. It's not for ever – and there is the bonus."

"I suppose..." replied Stella, "but I still wouldn't have agreed to it if it hadn't been implied that it would damage my prospects to be difficult about it. I don't feel at all comfortable with them in my apartment. Oh, hell – I really need a drink."

CHAPTER
NINETEEN

By the time they reached the bar, dusk had fallen with its usual suddenness, leaving a bar of liquid gold along the horizon the only remnant of the day. The hubbub in the bar burst on them as they entered. It was the end of the working week and most of the camp-based staff were there. Stella's spirits rose immediately.

"There's Hod," she said, pointing to a side table where Hod sat, a line of cans at his elbow. "Let's go over."

"Do we have to?" Trenhaile would have preferred to have Stella to himself tonight.

"Oh, go on – I want to know how he's getting on with his robots. He's probably more natural with them than we are."

"I think I'm OK with mine," Trenhaile offered as he followed Stella to Hod's table.

"Hi guys." Hod seemed genuinely pleased to see them. "How're ya doing – can I get you both a drink?"

"That's OK," Trenhaile responded with a proprietary hand on Stella's shoulder. "I know what Stella wants – and…" regarding the row of cans, "it looks as though you're OK for the time being." He departed for the bar, leaving Stella with Hod.

Stella weighed straight in with the questions she was dying to ask. "What are your robots like? How are you getting on with them?"

"Aw, they're fine. I'm kinda used to them anyway – though not at home, a'course. I don't pay much attention to them except for games – it's great to have something to really get my teeth into. They can always beat me, a'course, unless I tell them to hold back – but it's really sharpening my play."

"What did you get?" asked Stella. "I mean, which is the male and which the female?"

"They're neither really, yuh know," Hod explained, patiently for him. "It's only the way they look and the voice that makes ya think of them like that. Mine are both kinda male. More like a sorta room-mate situation."

"Oh," said Stella, surprised, "I thought we were supposed to have one of each."

"Yeah, well – I bent the rules a bit," Hod responded. "I think the bosses know I'm a special case. I know too much about these things for it to be a proper test with me, but I guess I may pick something up that you others won't. You can come back and see mine after if you like."

"I would, actually," said Stella. "I haven't worked out yet how to deal with this situation."

Trenhaile came back with the drinks to be greeted with, "Hey, Guy, how're you getting on with Adrienne – ain't she a cracker?"

Trenhaile looked slightly irritated, but his response, when he had put down the glasses, was masterly. "I thought she looked a lot like Stella and it would be nice to have a bit of Stella around when she was away at the pods."

Yes, me without the flaws, thought Stella, but all she said was, "Aah – that's pretty nice," and patted Guy's knee. "I just can't work out what happened with Boyd. These androids are programmed to please in every way – and they do, don't they?" This was directed at Hod.

"They sure are and they sure do." Hod smirked.

Stella saw an opportunity to get some technical insight into one of the issues that had been preying on her mind. "So how could Boyd get so angry with his android that he smashed her up? That's been worrying me quite a lot."

"Aw, I shouldn't worry about that." Hod smirked again, into his beer this time. "That was a one-off and he was a nutter." To Trenhaile: "I told you he had the hots for the android after we had dinner there. He didn't like her being nice to us as well."

"OK – I grant you that," said Trenhaile. "But surely she was programmed to smooth that sort of thing over and make it OK?"

Hod smirked again. "I really wouldn't worry about it. There's no way that kinda thing will happen again."

That's odd. How can he be so sure? thought Stella. *I wonder if he knows something he's not telling.* But Trenhaile had lost interest in the subject of Boyd and the conversation moved on to football.

The next round was Hod's, but when Trenhaile's turn came, and Stella and Hod were alone at the table, Stella went back to the subject.

"How can you be sure the Boyd thing won't happen again? I know you're an expert, but you can't possibly know that."

Hod took a last pull at the dregs in his glass. He seemed to be wrestling with himself.

"Look," he said. "Nothin' happens with these robots without us techies knowin' about it – we're in total control. Boyd's bots were my thing."

"But—" Stella didn't get to finish.

"Boyd was such a wanker – I just decided to have a bit of fun."

"My God," gasped Stella. "You're not saying—"

Hod interrupted her, looking more serious than she had ever seen him. "I'm not saying anything." The transatlantic lilt had gone, replaced by a hint of Essex. "Forget what I said – please?"

If that was what I think it was, thought Stella, *he must have messed with her program so she'd do something to provoke Boyd. I could get him the sack – Christ, he might even be charged with something.*

She was trying to decide what to reply when Trenhaile came back with the drinks.

"You two are quiet," he commented.

"Hod's been blinding me with science," said Stella, having made a quick decision. She noted Hod visibly relax as she said it. *I can't ruin someone just like that,* she thought. *He's just an immature idiot – and he won't do it again now he knows I know.*

But the atmosphere had changed. Hod and Stella were noticeably subdued. The life had gone out of the proceedings and the conversation faltered.

Something must have happened while I was at the bar, was Trenhaile's thought. *Perhaps he made a pass at her – I'll find out later.*

Finishing his drink, Trenhaile gave a nod to Stella. "I think we'll head off after this one, Hod," he said, standing up and noting that Hod made no attempt to detain them. Stella, too, seemed glad to leave.

She'll tell me what happened when I get her on her own, Trenhaile thought.

Leaving Hod to join the other techies in the bar, Stella and Trenhaile walked back towards Trenhaile's apartment with their arms round each other.

"The thing I can't get over out in Africa are the stars," said Trenhaile. "But we can't see them here for the camp lights – let's just walk out a bit now it's cooler and have a look."

"OK," said Stella, still a little quiet. *Should I tell him about Hod?* she was thinking. *No – I can't. He'd have to do something official about it.* However, it weighed on her mind and she couldn't relax, even when they lay down side by side to stargaze.

Trenhaile bent over to kiss her and she tried to respond.

"Is something up?"

"No – course not."

"It's no good saying that. I know you well enough now to know when something's worrying you."

"Don't worry," said Stella, getting up and brushing sand off her cargoes. "It's just a problem I've got at the pods and I can't stop thinking about it. Let's go to yours."

But inside Trenhaile's apartment she felt worse. Adrienne had appeared as they went in through the front door and offered drinks. Their usual form was to make straight for the bedroom, taking a bottle with them, but even Trenhaile, who had lectured Stella about her uneasiness around the robots, seemed to feel some constraint about progressing straight there.

"Another drink would be nice – what do you think?" to Stella.

I can't do this, thought Stella. "Actually I'm quite tired and I reckon I've had enough to drink. I think I'll head back and get an early night."

"Oh no – come on, you'll feel better after a real drink." Trenhaile came over and put his arm round her again. But she didn't relax into him – in fact she pulled away slightly.

"No, I really am tired." She almost shrugged him off.

"I'll walk you back then."

"No, don't be silly – it's only minutes away." *I have to be alone to think this through*, she said to herself, *and actually I do feel tired – very tired.*

She spoke so firmly that Trenhaile had to accept it.

Adrienne seemed to pick up on the tension. "Can I get you anything to make you feel less tired?" she offered solicitously.

I'm going to scream at one or both of them if I don't get out of here, thought Stella and, without saying anything more, she made for the door, not bothering to close it after herself.

Adrienne turned to Trenhaile. "I can see you're disappointed, Guy. Why don't you sit down and relax while I get you a drink? A long, cold beer or gin and tonic? Yes, beer – that's what I thought."

And Guy, giving up on the puzzle of Stella's mood, sank into his settee. *I'll see if Adie wants to sit and chat*, he thought. He had a work issue he wanted to mull over and he'd already found that her programming enabled her to respond intelligently when he discussed his work. Of course, she wasn't really thinking for herself, but it helped him to sort out his own ideas – and it was nice to have sympathetic company, even if it was, in fact, an illusion.

Stella was met at her own front door by Andrea. She could hear Hugo in the kitchen fiddling with something noisy.

"Good ev—" Andrea began, but Stella cut her short.

"I'm really tired and I think I'll go straight to bed."

"I'm sorry you're not yourself." There was real concern in Andrea's voice. "Would you like to sit and talk anything through? I can see something is worrying you. And can I fix you something to eat? You must be hungry."

I haven't eaten, thought Stella, *but how does she know? I certainly can't tell her what's worrying me.*

"I hope you'll let me know if I can do anything for you, Stella," Andrea went on. "You know Hugo and I are only here to help to make your life easier."

Does she know how I feel about them? And what do I mean by 'know'? Stella asked herself as she shut the bedroom door and threw herself on the bed.

CHAPTER
TWENTY

Isla's consulting room was next to the admin offices in the main building. Stella had never had any sort of therapy, and her ideas of what a consulting room would be like came exclusively from films. However, Isla's room gave no hint of any clinical purpose – it could have been the living room of one of the bohemian residents of Hampstead. Like Stella, she had softened the place with rugs and throws and there was no couch – rather a couple of stylish armchairs, a small settee and a slender sideboard against the wall, set with the paraphernalia for making coffee.

Stella had entered rather hesitantly and, at Isla's invitation to sit, had chosen one of the two armchairs arranged around a low coffee table.

"I wasn't expecting to see you as soon as this," Isla began conversationally. She went over to a sideboard under the window and returned with a tray already laid with cups and saucers and a full cafetière of black coffee. She sat down and crossed her legs, clad as usual in black, linen trousers. "Coffee?"

"Please," said Stella absently.

There was a pause as Isla filled the two white fluted cups and sat back.

"But I asked Mr Cooper to tell you all that you could come and see me any time, and I meant it – really, don't hesitate. Milk? Do help yourself – and sugar, if you take it."

Stella added milk to her coffee, ignoring the sugar. She sat awkwardly, apparently unsure as to how to begin.

"Is something worrying you?" Isla sat back, sipping her coffee, which she drank black.

Stella leaned forward, ignoring the coffee, hands clasped between her knees. "I feel quite stupid, really," she said. "It's about the robots – well, partly about that."

"I thought it might be." Isla had a pleasantly deep voice, reassuring without being in any way motherly. Her expression was professionally empathetic, displaying none of the appreciation of Stella as an attractive young woman that she had shown in Nairobi.

"I'm here to listen. Please go ahead and tell me about it."

"So, how's it going?"

Some two weeks after her first meeting with Stella, Isla Blair faced Cooper in his office. She and Cooper were seated in easy chairs, the standard URC executive coffee table between them. Cooper's large, lightwood desk, bare of papers, was positioned in another part of the room facing a panorama of desert scrub and vast, empty sky. Evidence of his status was apparent, in the size of the room, the sleek furnishings and colourful batik hangings on the walls. The tone of the conversation, however, was as between equals, his manner clearly acknowledging Isla's status as a professional.

"Well, I've seen all three of them twice now," Isla began, "and I'll be giving you full written reports after the third round of sessions, but I thought I'd just have a quick word now to raise something that may turn into an issue of concern. My initial assessment is that the men are coping well. Stella, on the other hand, is having problems."

"That's disappointing." Cooper leaned forward. "They were all pre-screened and judged psychologically robust. She is a scientist, after all. Are you saying that we've made a mistake in our selection – does she perhaps have vulnerabilities that the original assessment didn't pick up?"

"I wouldn't say that exactly. In fact, I would say that she's expressing concerns which are totally rational. These robots are intended to give the impression of being human. The men seem to be able to react and interact with them as if they were human while still thinking of them as machines. Stella, on the other hand, finds this dichotomy unsettling. That's in addition to her feeling that, for her, their unique properties, for instance that they can provide sophisticated services and be interactive companions, are unnecessary. Of course there may be some underlying unrelated insecurities and neuroses, but I would have to have more time with her to get to the bottom of those and anyway, I believe we still have to give serious attention to what she currently reports as her feelings about living with the robots."

"I see what you're saying." Cooper leaned back ruminatively. "We're hoping that there will be many uses for these robots, being a domestic companion is only one, and it may be that their therapeutic potential is one of their main uses in the end. Obviously these three are not needy in the sense that many potential customers will be, but before we start serious trials, which are inevitably going to mean publicity, we need to get a feel for how these products are going to work – and what is the best way to present them."

"I understand that," said Isla, "and I do think we can learn quite a lot from these three subjects who are…" she paused with a faint smile, "all very different. Stella, I think, feels more comfortable with the HU model, as it doesn't appear to be trying to be human. Male subjects seem to like the ANDs – for different reasons." The smile broadened. "The technician, O'Dwyer, is a special case. Because he's involved in the robots' design, he doesn't attribute any human characteristics to them at all. They really are just machines to him – but he's not typical. I personally don't have any reason to think there's cause for concern about the robots as products – although of course I'm relying on the advice of the technicians here – and I don't have any worries at present about the long-term psychological effects on the subjects in the current trial, but the differences in responses, particularly between male and female are…" she paused again, "interesting. As I said, we must take Stella's responses seriously. It would be easy to dismiss them as emotional and subjective, but I believe to do that would be a mistake."

"I'm sure you're not trying to say that men are more rational than women." This was said with a smile.

"Quite the contrary," was Isla's response. "I would say that Stella's reaction to the robots is entirely rational. There is one thing that did come up in my sessions with her which I wanted to explore with you at this stage. Is there any suggestion that the robots can…" she hesitated, "read minds – or communicate with each other?"

Cooper visibly relaxed. "Good heavens, no – none whatsoever."

CHAPTER
TWENTY-ONE

It was a relief to Stella to get back to the pods.

Andrea had packed for her, and she had to admit to herself that it was very nice not to have to worry about making sure all the washing and ironing was done and her desert boots waxed and ready for the trip.

Trenhaile had been surprisingly philosophical about her departure, despite the fact that it was some time since they had spent the night together or, indeed, had sex.

Thinking about this fact during the flight out to camp, Stella realised that, without making any conscious decision, she had lately been making various excuses to avoid intimacy.

Am I going off him? she asked herself, a question which she was unable to answer.

In fact, after their initial encounter in Nairobi, Stella and Trenhaile had progressed quite quickly from mutual attraction to discussion of plans for the future – return to the UK and possibilities for moving in together and pursuing their respective careers in London.

So what had caused the relationship to stall? It couldn't have been the robots, surely – although, thinking about it, their arrival had more or less coincided with the sex petering out. It was true that Stella felt inhibited by the presence of the robots in their respective apartments, despite telling herself that this was ridiculous. She also found Trenhaile's attitude to the robots faintly ridiculous – he really did seem to interact with them as if they were human, particularly Adrienne, and she acknowledged to herself that, despite her best efforts, this had caused her to lose a little respect for him.

On the other hand, she felt – and Isla's counselling had failed to dispel her concern about this – that her own responses to the robots were probably irrational. If she was convinced, as she was, that they were not human but were machines, why was she so unsettled by them?

She had been assured by both Isla and Hod that the AND and HU were definitely not able to communicate non-verbally and were both under central control. The fact that Hod had been able to manipulate the behaviour of Boyd's android supported the latter suggestion. However, there had been a number of incidents which had made her wonder about the communication issues and that worried her. For instance, as she had been watching Andrea do the packing, she had suddenly thought of a stick she had picked up on past site visits which was useful for testing the ground.

She had intended to go and dig it out from the garage, but before she could do so Hugo had appeared at the bedroom door carrying the stick.

"I thought this might come in useful," he had said in the distinctive voice which seemed to resonate from deep inside his metallic body.

And then, before Stella could express surprise, Andrea had commended Hugo on anticipating the stick's usefulness. *Almost as if she had picked up on my surprise and uneasiness and was trying to reassure me and divert me from drawing any conclusions.*

A small incident. She wouldn't mention it to anyone else, just as she hadn't mentioned the others. Nevertheless, she couldn't forget any of them.

It was all too complicated to worry about now and, anyway, as the small plane wheeled over the campsite and bumped down onto the narrow landing strip at Camp Greenhouse, she could put the worries out of her mind for the time being. The robots out here were much simpler models. She had never felt the slightest concern in their presence.

As the plane jolted to a halt, she saw that Mike Cunningham was there to meet her. "Great to have you back. Need something new to talk about. What's going down at HQ?"

Stella laughed. "Oh, same old, same old – a few new people out from the UK. Some of the old-timers gone – Jerry Lister, for instance." She would have loved to have talked to him about the trial, but it had been made clear that discussion with anyone not involved would be a disciplinary offence.

"You've got the same tent," said Cunningham, gallantly shouldering her rucksack. "I expect you'd like a rest and a bit of a brush-up before supper. I'll put this in the tent for you."

Grateful for some time to herself, Stella settled into the tent. Having unpacked and set out her sleeping bag on the camp bed, she lay down in the blond half-light created by the canvas, meaning to catch a few minutes' rest. It was very hot and she was tired. She closed her eyes. The sounds of camp life went on around her, but she heard them as if at a distance. An insect buzzed and struck the side of the tent. Gradually she became aware of voices inside the tent – inside her head? Although she couldn't make out actual words, in some way she felt that they were discussing her.

"Who are you? What are you talking about?" she called out and tried to sit up. But she found she couldn't move. It was as if a heavy weight was pressing on her chest, squeezing the breath from her body. Struggling and panicking, Stella fought against it with all her strength until, just when she thought she must suffocate, she had the sensation of a gentle hand on her forehead, and the intolerable pressure bearing down on her was lifted.

A voice, not identifiable as either male or female, said quite clearly, "You must not be afraid. You are in our hands – we will keep you safe."

She woke with a jerk, dry-mouthed and sweating, having rolled off the camp bed onto the hard floor of the tent.

"Christ, that hurt," she complained, sitting up and rubbing her back. She sat for a moment to recover, then, still shaken by the realism of the dream, she stood up unsteadily and staggered out of the tent. *I'd better have a shower and wake up properly. This robot thing is starting to get to me. It's not healthy. I need to get stuck into work.*

Cunningham was waiting as the freshly showered Stella made her way to the main tent.

"Sorry about that," she offered. "I didn't mean to fall asleep. I was more tired than I thought, and I really needed to shower and change to freshen up."

"That's fine," was the response. "I thought we'd just have a general review of the old pods today, but tomorrow I wanted to take you out to unit 6 – the new one out beyond the ridge. I think it's all going fine, but we may have to review the hydration timetable. I think some of the crops are getting too much."

CHAPTER
TWENTY-TWO

Stella and Cunningham set off early the next day in the cool hour just before sunrise. Unit 6 was some distance from the camp on the other side of a steep ridge. The horizon was streaked with pink and gold as they reached the top of the ridge and looked down on the pods, gradually resolving out of the gloom, like a clutch of translucent eggs.

"They always remind me of frogspawn," said Stella, laughing. "Did you ever go ponding for it when you were little?"

"Absolutely I did," said Cunningham. "My first foray into biological experiment. I won't tell you what I did with the frogspawn."

"No, don't. Poor little embryos," said Stella. "The bots don't look like tadpoles, though – wrong shape." And they both regarded the cuboid robots already rolling between the pods to effect the hydration.

"Better get down and take a look so we can get back to camp before it gets too hot," suggested Cunningham, and they scrambled down the slope, slippery with scree.

Once Cunningham had shown Stella a couple of sample pods and explained his concerns, they split up to complete the inspection. The air was completely still, the only sounds the hum and click of the robots as they went about their tasks and the soft crunch of her own footsteps on the dusty ground. A solitary kite wheeled silently overhead. Stella found herself at the farthest extremity of the site and was bending over to check a gauge when she heard a low growl.

Straightening up, initially she could see nothing but was aware of Cunningham gesticulating and shouting at her from near the base of the ridge.

She couldn't hear what he was saying but, turning round, realised that it was a warning. Half-crouched not more than a few yards away from her was a lion, a female who, from the way her bones stood out from her sides, appeared to be starving.

All operatives had been trained to deal with such situations, but Stella's mind was for a moment a complete blank of fear. When she recovered herself a little, she remembered that she must not run but must stand and face the animal and make loud noises to scare it off.

Her voice to her own ears sounded thin and wobbly, and the lion showed no signs of being intimidated. It merely crouched lower and, with a continuous growl, began to creep towards her.

It had covered a few feet, and Stella's shouting and gesticulating had petered out in despair when she became aware of a dark tide flowing, or rather rolling, between the pods towards the lion. The robots which had been attending to the pods had assembled and were advancing on the predator. The lion reared and started to back away before turning and disappearing into the distance.

Cunningham arrived at a run, breathless, in time to see it go. Within minutes, the robots had dispersed and resumed their duties. Apart from the emotional state of the humans, limp with relief, it was as if nothing had happened.

"My God – are you OK?" Cunningham gasped, putting a hand on Stella's arm.

"I reckon I'm lucky," she said when her breath returned. "But what was that with the robots?"

"I've never seen anything like it," said Cunningham quietly. "Never seen them do anything not connected with the pods – didn't know they could."

Stella seemed to sag and for a moment squatted on the ground, her hands over her face. Cunningham squatted down next to her and put his arm round her shoulders.

"I think I'd like to go back now," said Stella. "Sorry to be a wimp, but I need to sit down – somewhere safe."

"Of course – me too." Cunningham sounded equally shaken. "I've always wondered whether we shouldn't be armed."

"Wouldn't be any good to me," said Stella, her voice still shaky, as they walked back to the Land Cruiser together, taking nervous looks around them as they went. "I'm pretty sure I couldn't shoot anything, even if I knew how to use a gun."

"I reckon you could if it was you or the lion," said Cunningham.

"As a matter of fact, I don't think I could – even then," was her reply.

For the next few days, the team was on high alert, but the lion did not reappear and Stella was able to complete her work. What nagged at her mind, far more than the lion, however, was the behaviour of the robots.

Sitting by the campfire with Cunningham the night after the encounter, Stella fell silent, watching the sparks whirling madly upwards to a velvet sky, as always blazing with stars. The illuminated faces of the rest of the team, sitting around chatting quietly after their meal, seemed to float, strangely detached from their bodies.

"Are you OK?" asked Cunningham. "You're very quiet. I guess you had a nasty shock."

"I did," said Stella. "I certainly had a bad fright, but it's not that that I keep thinking about. It's the robots."

"Weren't they great?" said Cunningham with a laugh. "Thank goodness they were there."

"Yes – but why did they do it?"

"Well – as we're told, they're programmed not to allow a human to come to harm."

"But surely that's the advanced models – these are only programmed to water the plants in the pods."

The issue clearly didn't interest Cunningham. "That's a question for the tech boys – perhaps they program that into all of them."

"Sometimes I feel they're more than machines," Stella ventured. "They seem to me to be, well, almost human – in fact perhaps a bit better than that."

Cunningham considered the point seriously. "Well, personally, as a biologist I think that's unlikely. Don't you, if you really think about it? We know that human intelligence has multiple components – computational ability, spatial awareness, analytical reasoning, empathy – all the result of complex genetics. It's Hsu's view, isn't it, that human intelligence is likely to be impacted by as many as ten thousand genetic variants – so I just can't believe that any man-made machine could go near to replicating that."

"I suppose you're right." Stella felt unable to dispute the analysis as a biologist and didn't want to forfeit Cunningham's respect for her professionalism.

"I can understand that having humanoid robots in the house might feel a bit uncomfortable until you got used to them, though," Cunningham went on. Then, clearly anxious to lighten the mood, he turned to Stella, smiling. "To change the subject, how long are you planning to be out here – in Kenya, I mean? I'm hoping to get back to the UK in about a year."

Oh – is he going to hit on me? wondered Stella. Already accustomed to approving male attention back home, she had found that her appeal had increased dramatically in the camps, where women – particularly young, attractive, heterosexual women – were at a premium.

"Well, I don't see myself being here for more than another year or two," she said, "although it may depend on what Guy decides to do – that's Guy Trenhaile. We have talked about trying to get a joint posting back to the UK."

"Ah – the HR man." Cunningham took the point. "For myself, I'm thinking another year. I'm starting to feel like putting down some roots, and that would have to be back home – for me, anyway."

"Me too," from Stella, thinking, *That's got that out of the way*. Although they continued to talk about future plans, only half her mind was engaged. The other half was still on the conundrum of the robots. *I can ask Hod*, she thought. *I have to get to the bottom of it. They saved me; I should feel reassured – why does it make me feel uneasy?*

CHAPTER
TWENTY-THREE

Back at Camp Zebra, the first thing Stella did was to leave her kit with the staff at the bar. She then took her mobile out to the camp perimeter and phoned Hod. Each apartment was linked to the camp communications system, so she could have made her call from her apartment but, although she would have hesitated to explain her reasons to a third party, she preferred not to make it where the robots might be able to hear it.

"Hi Hod, I'm back."

"Stella – good to hear you. How's it going out there?"

"Hod – you heard about the lion and the robots?"

"Sure did. Pretty hairy stuff."

"I can't understand how the robots knew to do that."

"Well, ta be honest, it was a surprise ta us too. We went back to their programming and haven't got to the bottom of it."

"Well, is it something we should be worried about?"

"Worried? Hell no – why should we worry if they're better than we thought?"

"But I thought you said they were limited by their programs. Surely those robots should be limited to their hydration duties."

"Well, a' course there is their underlying programming – you know, the three rules – and maybe they were protectin' the pods – we did look at it. Ya really needa calm down, Stella. We know what we're doin'. How about leavin' it to us?"

And Stella felt she had to leave it there – for the moment, anyway.

It seems to be just me, she said to herself as she collected her kit and walked back to her apartment. *I've got to stop obsessing about it.* But the worry was still there, at the back of her mind.

Andrea and Hugo were at the door to meet her as she returned to the flat.

Andrea spoke for both. "We hope you've had a productive trip, Stella."

"Yes indeed," from Hugo. "How are the crops coming along?"

"Fine," said Stella shortly. *This is ridiculous*, she thought. *What's the point of having a conversation with a machine?*

"Can we help you unpack? There'll be some washing to do, I guess." Hugo moved towards the bedroom where Stella had left her rucksack.

Well, at least I don't have to bother to be polite, thought Stella, and said out loud, "Yes – do that will you, Hugo." But she felt uncomfortable being so short with them.

In order to give Andrea something to do and get her out of the way, Stella asked for tea and sat down in front of the communications box to contact Trenhaile. "Hi, I'm back," she said as soon as his face came into view.

"Hi there." His greeting was enthusiastic. "Great to have you back. Missed you a lot. Come over as early as you can and I'll get Adrienne to knock us up something." Was it Stella's imagination or was Adrienne hovering behind him in the room?

"I think I'd rather catch something in the bar," said Stella. "See you there at about 7.00."

As she put the receiver down, she found Andrea standing behind her. "Stella – Hugo and I could make something for you and Guy in the apartment and then switch off and leave you alone if you'd prefer."

She knows how I feel about them, thought Stella. *Why does that make me feel so uncomfortable? It doesn't seem to worry anyone else.*

"That's OK, Andrea. I just feel like going out tonight."

Andrea smiled and replied soothingly, "Of course, Stella. If there's anything else you want Hugo and me to do tonight, just let us know. That's what we're here for – to make you comfortable – and keep you safe."

I've heard those words in that voice before – recently, thought Stella, but she couldn't place the context and forgot about it as she went to have a shower and make herself presentable for Trenhaile.

The bar was very crowded and Stella realised that she wanted to be alone with Trenhaile – really alone – without either people or robots. "Can we get something to take away and go and eat it outside? It's cool now – I know it'll be cold later but I've got a jacket. I'd like to be alone – just the two of us."

Trenhaile smiled indulgently, flattered but also faintly irritated. He understood her reluctance to come to his apartment and felt that it was irrational. "That's sweet, but you know we can be alone in the apartments – you must try to stop thinking of the robots as people." He had been hoping for an early trip to the bedroom to celebrate their reunion.

"That's what everyone tells me, and I'm trying, but there's something about the HUs and the ANDs which makes it difficult. I've never had that feeling with the working robots – well, not until recently," she said reflectively.

Trenhaile got to the front of the queue and ordered cans and sandwiches. "OK – let's go – you choose the spot."

The camp was surrounded by a high wire fence, but beyond it there were concrete seats for camp inhabitants to sit and relax or watch the games, organised or spontaneous, that were a regular form of relaxation for inmates.

Stella and Trenhaile went out through the gates and sat on one of these seats facing the horizon, now layered orange and red by the setting sun.

"Did you hear about what happened out at the pods?" Stella began.

"I did – you know you guys should have guns. It's too dangerous for you to be out there virtually unprotected."

"Some camp personnel do have guns – I guess that's how Boyd got hold of one – but not usually the biologists, and I wouldn't want one," Stella replied with emphasis.

"Well, thank goodness for the bots."

"Well, that's one of the things I wanted to talk to you about. Don't you think it's spooky what they did to protect me – without any command from a human? I spoke to Hod and Cunningham about it, but it doesn't seem to worry them. Surely those sorts of robots can't think – reason?"

Trenhaile was clearly failing to empathise with such concerns. "Surely it's just something to be grateful for. I don't know anything about how the bots work or are programmed – I don't need to. After all, I don't know how a car works, but I can drive it. If Hod's not worried, I'd have thought that should put your mind at rest."

"Hod's judgement may not always be that good," said Stella darkly, thinking of the trick he'd played on Boyd.

Trenhaile laughed. "Granted, he needs to grow up a bit – like a lot of the tech boys – but I reckon there's nothing he doesn't know about robots. I'm still trying to understand what your problem with the HUs and the ANDs is. I can tell you don't really like having them around. It's ruining our sex life. We'll end up having it off outside and I'll be getting mosquito bites and sand and gravel in where the sun don't shine."

Suddenly Stella was desperate for Trenhaile to understand. "I don't really care what any robotics expert says; I have the feeling that the HUs and the ANDs – how can I say this – have a lot more going on inside than anyone thinks. Sometimes I get the impression they know what I'm thinking

— and I'm absolutely sure they can communicate with each other without speaking. And no one can explain why the field robots behaved as they did."

"I honestly haven't noticed anything like that myself." Trenhaile was anxious not to belittle Stella's fears but clearly couldn't relate to them at all.

"Look, I'm a biologist, not a robotics technician," said Stella. "Perhaps that's why I can't get the idea out of my head that we may have set something going that we're not in control of."

"What do you mean?" Trenhaile tried to keep his scepticism out of his voice.

"Well, obviously you know about human evolution. How can we be certain that by creating robots with sophisticated brains we haven't created something which can evolve?"

"The way it's always been explained to me," said Trenhaile patiently, "is that we should look at them as just another smart appliance. You don't expect the freezer to evolve just because it can turn itself on and off. I know you're worried, baby." He put an arm around her and pulled her to him. "But I genuinely don't think you need to be. Why not have another chat with Isla? That's what she's there for. I'm really out of my depth here."

"OK, I'll do that," said Stella, trying to keep the disappointment out of her voice. "Right." She briskly got up and dusted herself down. "Let's get back to yours and say 'Hello' properly."

But her heart was no longer in it.

CHAPTER
TWENTY-FOUR

ISLA BLAIR TO MIKE COOPER, 27 JUNE 2015

PRIVATE AND CONFIDENTIAL
SECURITY LEVEL A1
SUBJECT: Geneva Project

Introduction

I have now seen each subject three times over a period of six weeks and feel able to make preliminary assessments of the impact of the trial in the case of each.

My initial assessments are as follows:

Guy Trenhaile

Guy is a thirty-four-year-old HR professional, management grade 5.

He is a graduate of Edinburgh University and is a member of the Chartered Institute of Personnel and Development.

He has been with URC in Africa for four years, having been recruited at Grade 3 and achieved promotion to Grade 5 by applying for, and being appointed to, the position of head of human resources for the East African Division two years ago.

Guy's parents are professional people: father a solicitor, mother a teacher. They live in the UK. Guy, who is the middle child and only boy in a family of three, was educated at the local day grammar school. He is fond of his parents and maintains regular contact with them.

Guy has a superficially outgoing personality and is intelligent and articulate. He is not inclined to introspection, however, and, like many males, finds it difficult to talk about his feelings. He told me he had had no reservations about agreeing to participate in the Geneva Project and regarded it as something which could improve his career prospects within URC.

Guy's choices with regard to the physical appearance of the robots was interesting. He found it difficult to explain why he had chosen a female appearance for the realistic-looking android. His response was to the effect that it was nice to have something around that was 'easy on the eye'.

The HU model he thought of as male, although he was unclear as to why this was, as he admitted that neither the robot's appearance nor voice appeared to have been clearly gendered.

Guy's initial account of his reaction to living and interacting with the robots was wholly positive. He seemed to regard the HU merely as a sophisticated appliance which performed efficiently, and he apparently speaks to it only in order to give commands. This is despite the fact that it has been programmed to interact with him socially and, like the android, has also been equipped with the ability to discuss topics which Guy had identified to the technicians as of interest to him.

The android, on the other hand, appears to be regarded by Guy as almost human. He always refers to it by the name it has been given, Adrienne – or sometimes by the nickname he has given it 'Adie', and clearly has long conversations with it. He speaks with appreciation of its skill in making the flat comfortable and uses phrases such as, "It's quite nice to have a little feminine influence around the place and I can discuss work with her." I noted that he always refers to the android as 'her'.

Although not directly relevant to this study, I note that Guy is in a relationship with Stella Mayfield, one of the other subjects in this trial.

Assessment

As far as this subject is concerned, the android appears to have value as a companion. My assessment is that its value in this regard is linked to its humanoid appearance, and, it has to be said, to its apparent gender. There were also hints in the subject's replies that the 'stunning' appearance of the android and the fact that it was programmed to respond unquestioningly to the subject's needs were major factors in the approval rating.

There was certainly no indication in any of the interviews that Guy found either robot sinister or that he felt any uneasiness in having them as domestic companions. His rating of them was wholly positive.

The only long-term concern that I might have, were I to be in a clinical relationship with Guy, would be that there might be a tendency here to confuse the apparent humanity of the android with reality. In other words, to regard the android as a real, and indeed 'perfect', human being. Since no human would be able, or indeed want, to achieve the type of total compliance and congeniality that these robots have been programmed to exhibit, this would have the potential to have a deleterious effect on his social and intimate relationships with other humans.

Henry O'Dwyer

Henry (who prefers to be called 'Hod') is a senior robotics engineer aged twenty-eight.

He studied robotics at Southampton University and joined URC as a trainee immediately on leaving university.

He has been based in Camp Zebra for eighteen months and applied to be posted to Africa 'to do something different and get some excitement'. He enjoys the work at this base, particularly on the development of the humanoid robots, but finds camp life 'kind of dull'.

Henry is the youngest of a family of five and grew up in Essex, UK. His father is a builder and his mother a housewife. Henry is fond of his parents and siblings but admits that he is not good at being in regular contact with them. He tends to socialise mainly with the other technicians in the camp, although he is also friendly with the pilots who are based here.

Henry is very influenced by American culture and adopts a transatlantic accent. Computers are the focus of his interest and have been since he was a child. Much of his relaxation involves internet-based social media and computer games. He has an ambition to invent a successful computer game and 'clean up'.

Henry regards the robots as 'pieces of kit'. He is no doubt influenced in this by the fact that he was closely involved in their programming and part of his day job is to monitor the performance of all the robots operating in the project and intervene to correct any malfunctions.

Although he acknowledges that the trial brief was that all three subjects should choose gendered robots at least for the android, he does not speak about either his AND or HU as if they were human or had a gender identity, and his only social interaction with either appears to be to pit himself against them in computer games. He does, however, have some idea of being able to use one or both of them to assist him to develop a ground-breaking new game. He is perfectly comfortable with having the robots in his living quarters and cannot understand how they could cause anxiety.

Assessment

This subject is not one for whom face-to-face social interaction is of high importance to his wellbeing. The ability of the robots to free him from any domestic tasks and to participate in the activities which interest him is of value to him and undoubtedly contributes to his toleration of the necessarily limiting nature of camp life.

He is totally at home with robots and artificial intelligence in general, humanoid or otherwise, and finds the idea that they might be felt to be sinister or unnatural incomprehensible.

My clinical concerns for Henry relate to a tendency, which is already highly developed in him, to find his reality in the world of artificial intelligence rather than that of human affairs. When asked when he thought it would be appropriate to turn the appliances and robots in his home off, Henry could not think of any situations in which he would wish to do so. My long-term concern for Henry as a patient would be a gradual disengagement from the 'real world' and a loss of the type of social connections and interactions that we know to be important to mental health.

Stella Mayfield

Stella is an agronomist, Technical Grade 7, and is aged twenty-seven.

She is a graduate of King's College, Cambridge, and joined URC three years ago, having completed a PhD focusing on plant culture in desert environments at Imperial College, London.

She applied to be posted to Project Greenhouse in East Africa to gain experience in this cutting-edge science and because she 'believes passionately' in the importance of the work being done. Stella is the younger child of parents who have recently retired from academic posts, one as a biologist and one a physicist. She has an older brother who is currently studying in the United States. Stella and her brother have no memory of their natural father who left the family soon after Stella was born and lost contact when they were young. They have been legally adopted by their stepfather, with whom they both have an affectionate relationship. Stella is close to her family and speaks regularly to her parents and brother on Skype. She regards her time in Africa as an exciting opportunity but is confident that her long-term future will be a more settled life in the UK. She has in the past found the limited social and cultural life at the camp difficult at times but, since she has been in the relationship with Guy Trenhaile, this has ceased to bother her. She feels that the relationship has the potential to be long term.

Stella had concerns about the trial from the outset but understood the importance of it for the product and the company. I also received the impression that she felt that her agreement to take part was important for her career progression at URC.

Although Stella does not find it difficult to talk about personal matters, she was reticent when discussing her attitude to the robots assigned to her. I came to the conclusion that she felt that it would count against her professionally if she appeared to be unable to deal with the situation. She is also anxious not to appear emotional or neurotic, characteristics which she believes are often wrongly attributed to females.

What I was able to conclude from our sessions, however, was that she does not feel totally comfortable with either the AND or the HU. Stella is someone who does not feel herself in need of the potential benefits offered by these robots either in terms of companionship or practical assistance. She does appreciate being relieved of domestic chores on occasion but would often prefer to do these herself as she finds domestic routine a relaxing change from work and feels uncomfortable taking such tasks back from the robots. She conceded that this was irrational as she is entirely free to use or not use the robots as she chooses but explained the feeling by saying that she found it difficult to regard them as mere machines without feelings. She finds herself disinclined to discuss her work with either robot for reasons which she was unable to articulate.

Assessment

This subject's reaction to the experiment is the least positive. She does not feel that the robots are meeting a personal need and the fact that they can interact in simulation of human behaviour is to her a disadvantage rather than an advantage and something that she finds unsettling.

I do have clinical concerns about Stella's mental health. It is possible that the interaction with the humanoid robots is bringing to the fore suppressed insecurities and anxieties. Although reluctant to say so in terms, I gained the impression that she might be feeling that the robots can penetrate her mind, and the apparent perfection, particularly of the android, has brought out underlying feelings of inadequacy and insecurity that may have been present and suppressed for a long time.

This was the set of interviews which I found least satisfactory, since I came to the conclusion that I had not succeeded in eliciting from Stella the root cause of her unease and her inability to use the robots in the way intended. I hope to be able to resolve this issue in future sessions.

As agreed, I will be sending a further report in four weeks' time.

CHAPTER
TWENTY-FIVE

Two days after her return from the pods, Stella sat in Isla's consulting room, hands twisting in her lap.

"As we weren't due to meet until next week, Stella, I assume that you have something specific you want to talk about." Isla sat back and waited for Stella to begin.

"It's not just one thing." Stella looked down at her hands, twisted into a ball on her knees.

"Do you want to go ahead and tell me about it? As you know, I'm here to listen."

There were several minutes of silence as Stella tried to marshal her thoughts. Faced with what she hoped would be a sympathetic ear, she felt herself welling up. She gripped the arms of her chair and said tearfully, "I'm almost starting to feel I'm going mad. No one else seems to feel about the robots as I do. Is it just me? Am I being neurotic?"

"Well," Isla's response was measured. "We have talked before about your discomfort around the robots. Why would you think that no one else feels as you do?"

"I know that Guy and Hod don't, and I have to admit that none of the robots I work with has ever bothered me before. I can't help thinking about what happened with the Boyds when this type of robot was introduced into their household." Stella paused. "Obviously something went wrong there, but then I gather from all the talk that the Boyds were considered 'odd and unstable', and I hope no one would ever apply those terms to me. And then…" she looked uncomfortable, "there might have been other reasons for what happened with Derek, Derek Boyd."

Isla leaned forward in surprise. "Do you know something about the circumstances of the incidents involving the Boyds that hasn't come out yet, Stella?"

"I can't say – I really can't, but I don't think anything that happened with the Boyds has any bearing on my feelings. I just can't feel that the HUs and the ANDs are only machines."

"Let's go back to the basics of what we know," said Isla gently. "Firstly, robots are man-made. I'm not a roboticist so, like you, I have to rely on what the experts tell me, but doesn't it make sense when we're told that, because the robots are machines made and programmed by humans, they only have those powers which the technicians give them?"

"Of course that makes sense," Stella was beginning to sound tearful again, "but I just can't make myself believe it. I used to have no problem with the more basic robots, but since the incident out at the pods, I've found myself looking at them in a different way – trying to work out what's going on inside them."

"Of course, I know about the incident at the pods," said Isla. "It's understandable that it should have shaken you up. But why did it make you worry about other robots?"

"Well, I've never seen the robots at the pods do anything other than their pre-programmed tasks. These acted totally differently – and how did they know what to do, or even that there was a need to do it?"

"Is that not something to do with the basic programming of all robots?"

"That's what Hod said when I asked him about it, but it doesn't seem to me to explain it – it was so outside their basic programmed tasks – and…" Stella hesitated, "I had had a dream."

Now Isla's attention was seriously engaged. "A dream? Can you tell me about it?"

"Well, it's hard to describe exactly. It was more of a feeling – and I did think I heard voices," said Stella. "I felt a terrible pressure, as if I was suffocating and then… then… a voice telling me that I was being looked after and the pressure eased."

"And how did that make you feel?"

"Well, I'm not sure why exactly, but I felt it was one of the robots talking to me – I mean one of my robots, Andrea or Hugo – and it made me feel frightened."

"Frightened?"

"I know it seems odd – if they were telling me that they would look after me – but…" she paused and looked down again," it made me feel as if I had no control – was in the hands of something else. And then the robots at the pods behaved completely out of character – oh, I know they saved me – but it was sort of the same thing and they aren't supposed to be able to do that."

"Do you think, perhaps," Isla put in gently, "that you're transferring your worries about the humanoid robots to all robots? How did you feel about the robots at the pods before?"

Stella's hands went to her head. "Absolutely fine. To me before they've always been just part of our tool kit. But after the incident with the lion I feel differently about them. Wary, I suppose. If I start to be nervous of them it's going to affect my work. It's a disaster – and," hesitantly, "it's affecting my personal relationships." She paused. "Well, with Guy, Guy Trenhaile."

"Do you want to talk about that?"

Stella sounded embarrassed. "I suppose it's two things. I've tried to talk to him about my nervousness around Andrea and Hugo, and his robots – and the thing at the pods – and I can tell he just thinks I'm being neurotic, so I've given up. But also…" She hesitated again.

"Yes?" Isla leaned forward.

"I can't help thinking that he treats his android like a real person – he talks about her in that way. And this is ridiculous, I know, but I almost feel jealous sometimes – she's so gorgeous to look at and so eternally charming. I can't compete with that!"

"Hmm," Isla said thoughtfully. "It's really all part of the same problem, which is your tendency to attribute real humanity to the robots. And from what you've told me today, these feelings are becoming more acute." After a pause, "How would you feel if I recommended to Cooper that you should be taken out of the study? My main concern has to be your health."

Stella was sufficiently aware of the danger of being identified within the company as a neurotic female for this suggestion to induce panic. "Please don't do that," she said, agitated. "I know I've got to go on with it, and I can cope, I really can. You're right – I have to rely on the experts. And talking to you helps – it really does."

"If you're sure, Stella. I'm pleased these sessions help. But your mental health is my priority and we'll have to see how it goes. If you think you can make it through the final weeks, I'll go along with that, but I am concerned. The important thing to realise is that you can come and talk to me any time in complete confidence. To me, your fears seem perfectly natural even if they're unnecessary. I'm sure we can come up with some strategies to help you deal with them."

"That would be good." Stella tried to sound relieved but she was thinking, *It isn't any good trying to convince anyone else. I'm on my own. I've just got to try to get through this. Perhaps they're all right and I'm imagining things.*

After Stella had gone, Isla sat for some time thinking through the interview before writing up her notes.

Then she picked up the phone.

CHAPTER
TWENTY-SIX

Trenhaile thought it would be a romantic gesture when his and Stella's leave came up if he took her back to Nairobi where they had first become a couple.

Though not overly given to introspection, he had sensed a constraint in Stella's manner towards him, particularly since her return from his latest trip to the pods, and had been worrying about how to overcome it. After some reflection and an uncharacteristically revealing discussion with Isla, he had decided that the most likely cause was Stella's struggle with the home robot experiment. Apart from her obvious unease in the presence of her own robots, she seemed to have a particular antipathy to his android, Adrienne. She had become reluctant to go into his apartment at all and became noticeably irritated when he mentioned Adrienne, especially since she had realised that he had given Adrienne the nickname 'Adie'. He admitted to himself that he might have been inclined to talk about Adie rather a lot in the first flush of enthusiasm for the experiment. As far as he was concerned, the experiment had turned out to be a totally positive experience – well, insofar as it affected his domestic arrangements. However, you couldn't say the same about its effect on his relationship with Stella. Their sex life had dwindled to almost nothing since the arrival of the robots. That was very depressing. Even before he had met Stella, Trenhaile had begun to feel that the time was approaching when he should think about returning to put down roots in the UK and start a family – perhaps not immediately, but in the next year or two. And, until recently, he had actually felt that Stella might be 'The One' to do it with.

He did – yes, he did – love her, and she was perfect for him in so many ways: intelligent, sociable, adventurous, physically extremely attractive; she was all he could imagine wanting in a life partner. But he had to admit to himself that things were not going well. How could he revive what they had first had together? It was definitely worth a big effort to save this relationship.

Stella had reacted to the suggestion of a trip to Nairobi with enthusiasm, almost with relief. "Oh, yes, please. I can't wait to get away from the camp for a few days and I do miss the bright lights – even if it's only Nairobi and not London," was her immediate reaction.

There was no question in Trenhaile's mind of returning to the dreary Lone Impala. He had chosen the most expensive hotel he could afford in Westlands for the scene of romantic re-connection. Ensconced in their silkily luxuriant suite – a symphony of beige, cream and gold – they made love as rapturously as on their first night in the Impala.

It's going to be OK, thought Trenhaile, lying back and lazily stroking the smoothness of Stella's shoulder.

He rolled over to kiss her. "That was wonderful." He paused. "I was starting to get worried about us but – it's all right, isn't it?"

Stella turned towards him and gave him a swift kiss. "Of course it's all right. I just needed to get away for a bit. This was a brilliant idea, Guy – I do love you." This was said lightly, almost flippantly, but Guy chose to follow it up.

He leaned over Stella and cupped her face, still flushed with the afterglow of sex, in his hands. "I know you said that casually, Stella, but I'm going to say something I've been thinking for some time. I think I am in love with you. I think we're really good together and I want to know if you feel the same way. I'm sure we could make a good life together – if we're on the same page, it's what I'd want."

Stella sat up and hugged her knees. "I think it could work," she said carefully, "but I've been thinking a lot about my future, and I've come to the conclusion that I need a change of direction. I don't want to work around robots anymore – and I'd like to go back to the UK."

"Me too." Trenhaile lay back on the pillows with his hands behind his head. "I thought we could do another year or two out here to get together a deposit for a house, and then both apply for transfers back."

"No, Guy," said Stella quietly. "I can't wait two years – and I need to move from URC. I'm as committed as ever to the environmental projects, but I don't want to work with robots or have anything to do with the company's other projects going forward."

"Oh, but it's so easy to save out here – we could really get a stack of money together."

"Sorry, Guy – that's how I feel." Stella's face was set in an expression which Guy recognised, and it warned him to back off the subject. This was an area that was non-negotiable.

"Look," he said, "our relationship is more important to me than money or even saving for a house. If that's the only basis on which we can be together – we'll have to try to work things so we can do that. You might have to go back before me, but I'm sure I can find something on at least the same money in the UK – I'll have to change companies if necessary."

"Oh, Guy." Stella turned and nestled her face into the hollow of his neck. "I wasn't sure you'd react like that. I do love you, I really, really do."

Guy had decided that the most romantic thing they could do was to return to Habesha to try to recapture some of the excitement of their first evening together. It had been an inspired choice. Sitting together in the velvet dark, fragrant with the scent of herbs and cooking, their faces illuminated by the glow of the fire pits, it was as if any problems between them had been left in the desert.

They had asked the taxi to drop them a little way from the hotel so that they could walk back, arms entwined, through the cool of the evening. Before going up to the room, they shared a sunlounger by the hotel pool, a translucent aquamarine, lit from below. It was late and they were alone, the only sound the grating chirp of the cicadas and the distant hum of traffic. Stella lay between Trenhaile's legs, leaning against him, her head tucked under his chin.

"Guy," said Stella softly. "Do you ever wonder about the future – not for us, I mean, but for humans? We're trying to green the desert here – and that's important as the world population explodes – but do you ever wonder where it will end? After all, thirty thousand years ago the entire human population of the world may not have been much more than a million."

"It may astonish you to know I don't," he responded, kissing the top of her head. "You're the biologist, not me. I'm just a simple male. My main worry is my future – and yours. I reckon the world I know will see me out."

Stella sat up and turned to him, suddenly serious. "I do think about it a lot – I can't help it. It's partly being out here – where they think we, homo sapiens, evolved, but it's also partly working with robots."

"Come on, darling." Trenhaile tried to pull her back to lie against him, but she resisted. "I brought you out here so we could get away from robots and you could forget about them and your worries for a bit."

"But think about it," Stella persisted, ignoring his plea and resisting his attempts to pull her back towards him. "Evolution has been speeding up – it took hundreds of thousands of years for us to evolve from Lucy in the Olduvai gorge to the first modern humans. Since then we've gone from living in caves to being able to transplant spare parts into ourselves – all in thirty thousand years."

"Thirty thousand years seems quite long to me," said Trenhaile; he tried not to sound flippant but was afraid of losing the romantic mood.

"In evolutionary terms it's not," said Stella earnestly, "but anyway, it's speeding up. For instance, originally, most humans, like other mammals, could only digest milk when they were infants, but nine thousand years ago people started herding animals rather than relying on hunting and a genetic mutation took place which enables most of us now to digest milk as adults. And skin colour – it's thought that until about ten thousand years ago European and African skin looked much the same, but then people living in the North who needed to absorb more of the UVB rays in the rarer sunlight developed lighter and lighter skin. But the big change is in the size of our brains. We don't have to wait for evolution anymore; we can use gene editing to by-pass it or speed it up. And we can create artificial intelligence – who's to say one day it won't be greater than our own?"

It was a long lecture, and Trenhaile was not in the mood for speculating about the future of humanity. He was anxious to preserve the romantic atmosphere. "Look," he said, gently taking her in his arms, "I'm an expert in people management, you're an expert biologist, but neither of us is an expert in robotics. We have to rely on the opinion of those experts, don't we? We have to respect their expertise – don't we?"

"But supposing biology and artificial intelligence have become, as it were, inter-connected. We've been top of the tree – we think we are in control, but supposing our large brains are enabling us to invent our own successors. When I speak to those humanoid robots and see them in operation, I can't think of them as just machines."

"But Stella – that's what they *are*. Come on, my love, you've got this totally out of proportion." He finally managed to take her in his arms. "Let's go to bed," he said, his mouth against her hair.

And she allowed herself to relax against him. *Perhaps I am neurotic*, she thought. *Perhaps I'm letting my imagination run away with me. I must get a grip. Guy's going to lose patience.*

CHAPTER
TWENTY-SEVEN

The flight back from Nairobi was bumpy. Stella was generally relaxed about flying and unfazed by turbulence, but she found herself longing for a drink on the short flight. She had to be honest with herself. *It's not the flight; it's the prospect of facing the robots again.*

She didn't feel she could say anything about this to Trenhaile. *He doesn't think there's anything in it. He'll lose patience with me, and it's all going so well. I only have to hang on for a few more weeks until the programme ends,* she thought. *And I'm going to start job hunting as from now.*

But as she entered her apartment, the feelings of unease returned in force despite the fact that there was no sign of the robots. That in itself seemed almost sinister.

The robots were in effect confined to the flat by their

programming, so their absence was surprising and, in her current frame of mind, unnerving. She went from room to room, searching and calling out to them, before finding them in the garage.

They were simply standing together against the outside wall. Stella felt foolish for the note of panic that had appeared in her voice as she searched and said, "Oh, there you both are. I was just wondering."

Andrea, who tended to act as spokesman for them both, came forward, saying gently, "We thought you'd like to be by yourself for a bit when you came back, Stella. We can stay out of the way in here if you like or come back into the flat if you prefer. Just let us know what you want."

What I want, thought Stella, *is not to have robots in my house.*

Almost as if in answer to that thought, Andrea added, "You don't need to worry about our feelings, Stella. Our role is to do exactly what you want us to do, so if you'd prefer us to make ourselves scarce," the colloquialism sounded odd delivered in Andrea's modulated tones, "we can stay in here until you are ready for us to come back into the flat."

Stella made an effort to speak normally. "No – it's fine. I'll unpack myself, but then if you and Hugo can deal with the washing and get something ready for supper – something light – I'll probably turn in early."

"Of course, Stella," the robots replied in unison, and they followed her back into the apartment.

Having unpacked, Stella sat down to the meal of curried goat and rice which Andrea had prepared and drank more than she intended of a bottle of Sancerre, cold from the fridge in the garage. Apart from serving her and then clearing the table, the robots stayed out of the way, although she could hear them moving about in the kitchen, no doubt washing up and doing the laundry.

Stella sat down in the living room to contact Trenhaile. They always spoke remotely if they didn't meet on any day.

"Thanks for a brilliant, brilliant time," she said. "I can't tell you how much I needed that. And, more seriously, don't you think it was what we needed – I mean, we as a couple?"

"It was wonderful." His voice dropped. "It will be a long time before I forget that room in the hotel. You were magic."

"I meant a bit more than that – it's the first time we've talked about the future really seriously." Stella felt it was important to keep the topic alive.

"Yes – but it's not the first time I've been thinking about it." *That was true, wasn't it?* Trenhaile reassured himself.

"I'm going to use tomorrow to start exploring the possibilities for getting back to the UK."

"OK, but perhaps we ought to talk it through a bit more before you speak to anyone else about it. It needs planning." Was there a hint of reservation in his voice?

"Of course we can do that, but I want to get on with it." She lowered her voice. "I've got to start doing something about it now, Guy – for my own peace of mind. Look – I've got three days at the pods coming up this week," she went on. "I'm going to have an early night tonight, but can we get together tomorrow evening – about 6.00?"

Better leave it at that for the moment – about the future, thought Guy. "Sure – no reason not to start exploring the options. I'll drop by for you at 6.00 tomorrow then," was all he said.

"Why don't I come and get you?" said Stella. "If I'm not there bang on six just wait for me."

She spent the next day on the internet exploring job opportunities in the UK. Although she worried that she hadn't made this completely clear to Trenhaile, she had already decided that she must leave, not only Africa but also URC. She had mentioned that before, but she knew he had not really accepted it. He would be disappointed. He liked the idea of her working for the same company as him and, of course, he thought it might make it easier to coordinate their careers. Perhaps it would be best to deal with the issues one at a time. A move to the UK first, then a job outside the company. On reflection, it didn't even have to be the UK they moved to.

The one thing I'm sure of, Stella said to herself as she scanned the vacancies, *is that I don't want to be around robots anymore.*

CHAPTER
TWENTY-EIGHT

Around 6.30, Stella arrived at Guy's apartment to collect him. She noted with the irritation she always felt, the touches outside his apartment introduced by the robots – well, Adrienne, she suspected – the pots of colourful succulents, the rustic wind chimes, the potted palm by the door and the cushions, rugs and lamps inside.

"It's nice to have some homely touches around the place," Trenhaile had said when the changes first appeared. "I'm not good at that sort of thing myself."

"I could have got some of those things for you," Stella had said when they first appeared.

"Oh, you've got a lot of other things to do – might as well use the robots for what they're good at," had been the reply.

What aren't they good at? Stella had thought.

No one locked their door at the camp and Stella had carte blanche to go into Trenhaile's apartment whenever she wanted, so she went straight in.

Guy and Adrienne were sitting together on the sofa talking quietly. Guy had a file open on his knee.

"Hi." He got up and came over to kiss Stella, who had stopped on the threshold.

I almost feel as if I'm intruding, she thought.

Her response was muted. "Ready, Guy?"

"Adie and I were just discussing a personnel issue that's come up with one of the engineers. I think we're done, aren't we, Adie?"

"I would say so," responded Adrienne, and got up, carefully reassembling the file and taking it to the filing cabinet in the corner of the room.

Trenhaile sensed a slight atmosphere but decided to ignore it. However, he realised it would be best to get Stella out of the apartment as quickly as possible. He put his arm round her and steered her out.

But he was thinking, *This is a pain. I'm getting fed up with it.*

Going out at camp meant going to the bar. The idea was to grab a quick meal; the choice was limited but it was OK, and then go out for a walk while it was cool. Trenhaile was hoping that he could persuade Stella back to stay the night at his place. He had even briefed the robots to be out of the way if he came back with her. He realised, however, it had been a blunder to let Stella find him in conversation with Adrienne like that. *It's ridiculous, but I've got to live with it for the moment. Why can't Isla help on this? It's definitely not normal.*

The intention, once in the bar, had been to find a corner and try to avoid socialising, but the bar was full and the corner they had been aiming for was occupied by Hod, uncharacteristically drinking on his own, staring into space with an untouched beer in front of him.

"Hod looks rather sad," said Stella. "I think we ought to go over and cheer him up – for a bit, anyway."

"Oh, God, do we have to? He's OK, I suppose, but I do find him a bit of a bore. And the 'America speak' gets on my nerves."

"Just one drink." Stella was determined. "And there's something I'd like to pick his brains about."

"Not robots!" Trenhaile's exasperation was clear. "Never mind – I'll get the drinks. What's yours? The usual?"

Hod seemed barely to notice when Stella sat down with him, and his reply to her greeting was a grunt.

After sitting in silence for a few minutes, Stella put a hand on Hod's shoulder. "Are you OK? You don't seem your usual self."

"I'm fine," he said, making an obvious effort to be sociable.

"I don't think you are, really. Want to talk about it?" Stella thought her own questions about the robots would have to wait.

"Just tryinna think it through. Some stuff going down at work."

"What is it? It's obviously worrying you."

"Well." He paused, and then decided to come clean. Stella was always a sympathetic listener and he felt more comfortable explaining his anxiety to a woman than he would to a man. "There's gonna be some changes in the way we work. We've always used computers, but the guys – well, me included – have developed some that they think can do all the design and build of the robots on their own."

"They'll still need to be programmed and supervised by you, though, won't they?" Stella's words suggested more reassurance than she felt.

"Well –as a matter a' fack not. These bots can program other bots, which can then develop their own programs. I guess I may be getting this whole thing out of proportion, but I suddenly started wondering where I'm gonna fit in when these bots come on stream."

Any idea of Stella asking the questions she had intended had gone out of the window with these revelations.

"Do you mean to say that these things are potentially autonomous? They don't need people at all?"

"In a way, yeah – you could put it like that."

"I'm not surprised you're worried." Stella was still trying to absorb the information.

"I guess I gotta starta think 'bout where I go from here."

"Does that mean these things are getting outside our control? Is that really a good idea? Isn't anyone worried about that?" Stella tried to keep her voice normal, but inwardly she was reeling with disbelief.

"Oh – I don' worry about that. All AI has ta protect and promote the wellbeing of humans – it's built in. Was really just thinkin' about where I go from here if my job disappears."

Stella felt ill-equipped to give any sensible reassurance, but she tried. "Well, personally, I'm looking for a change. I definitely want something new – even if it means re-training." There was no point in trying to explain her reasons to Hod.

"You're young, you've got no dependants, like me, you can do anything – go anywhere. Anyway, I can't believe techies like you are redundant yet."

"I guess you're right."

At this point Trenhaile returned with the drinks, and neither Stella nor Hod was inclined to continue the discussion in his presence. Hod seemed to have recovered himself a little, but he was definitely subdued and, without being rude, seemed indifferent as to whether Stella and Trenhaile stayed or went, so after one drink they left.

Outside the bar Stella tried to explain. "He's worried. Apparently there's some new AI which can more or less take over what he and the other techies do at present, so he thinks his job might be at risk." And then, as the idea dawned on her, "I guess you know about this already."

Trenhaile looked slightly uncomfortable. "I do know something about it. It's been under development for some time – actually, Hod had a hand in it himself."

"And are there going to be job losses?" Stella was not prepared to let him off the hook.

Trenhaile's discomfort increased. "There may be, but, you know, when technology takes over one job, other jobs are created."

"I'm not sure we've had to deal with anything like this technology before. These are more than machines – they're a new type of being."

"Oh, come on – people have always worried about new technology. Think about the machine breakers in the nineteenth century. But it's always ended up improving lives. Can we stop talking about this now? We need to get something to eat – it'll have to be in one of the flats if we don't want to go back in the bar with Hod there."

"OK," said Stella resignedly. "Let's go to yours. I'm sure Adrienne can knock us up a gourmet meal in no time."

Trenhaile decided to lighten the mood. "Miaooow! I do believe you're jealous!"

CHAPTER
TWENTY-NINE

The departure lounge at Nairobi airport was a colourful maelstrom – every skin shade and language was in evidence – a crowd in perpetual motion. All seats were taken, but Stella and Trenhaile managed to find a table in the restaurant. They sat opposite each other, trying to eat a meal neither really wanted.

"Suppose you don't get one of these jobs? Universal really rate you – I know you could get your job back." Trenhaile's voice had a pleading note.

"Guy," said Stella quietly. Trenhaile's hand was lying on the table and she covered it with her own. "When I'm sorted, you're going to follow." She paused. "Aren't you." It was a statement, not a question.

"Of course, of course, but it may not be easy finding

something at my level – I've shown you what's out there at the moment."

There was an awkward pause broken by Stella. "You know, I can't help feeling that if you really loved me, were really committed to our future together, you wouldn't worry too much about your job or salary. You'd want us to be together at any cost."

"But I am thinking about our future – and I can't help worrying about us giving up the chance to save for a deposit on a house. That *is* our future, isn't it?"

"Yes – but money's not the be all and end all. You know the reason I have to go, but, be honest – you think it's based on a neurosis, don't you?"

"You're not a neurotic person. You're one of the most intelligent people I know, and I love you. But I can't understand why you have to go – not now the trial has ended and you don't have to have the robots around anymore."

"They will be gone in a few days, I know, but I don't feel the same about any of the robots, and I have to work with the ones at the pods. I've explained all this. Surely you'll feel some sort of relief to have the apartment to yourself again, won't you?"

Trenhaile looked uncomfortable. "Well, actually, I've told Cooper I don't mind keeping the robots for a bit."

Stella became very still. "You *are* joking," she said. "You actually *want* to live with things that look and sound like humans but are machines. I know you don't find them unsettling like me, but for goodness' sake, your apartment's full of appliances – what do you need fake humans for?"

"I'm not going to lie to you, Stella. I've found being able to talk to Adrienne about work and things really helpful. Come on – can't we agree to differ on this?"

"Of course we can," said Stella carefully – and then, more slowly, "Yes – we certainly do differ," she added thoughtfully.

There was an uncomfortable pause and she went on, putting down her knife and fork and pushing away the half-full glass of wine. "I think I'll go through to departure now. Best not to drag it out – and I'm not really hungry, to be honest."

Trenhaile was alarmed. "The flight hasn't been called yet. Stella, come on – I want as much time with you as possible. I don't know when I'm going to see you again."

"Let's not drag it out. I'd rather go now – really." And she got to her feet decisively.

Trenhaile reluctantly followed her out of the restaurant, wheeling her suitcase.

After checking in her luggage, Stella faced Trenhaile by the entrance to the departure area.

He pulled her towards him, but she disengaged herself, not looking him in the eye.

"Stella," he said, a note of panic in his voice, "phone me as soon as you land. Promise!"

"Of course," was the reply, but her voice had no life in it. And then she did look at him. "Goodbye, Guy," she said, and turned to walk through the glass doors without looking back.

⁂

Guy's feelings were in turmoil on the flight back to camp. He had never felt about anyone before as he felt about Stella, but was it going to, could it, work out? Life at camp wouldn't be the same without her – could he hack it here for another year? As he parked and walked back through the camp, he found himself going over and over the various possibilities of their future together.

I don't know – I just don't know what to do… was his last thought as he reached his apartment.

He opened the door to a haven of calm and order. Adrienne was standing in the doorway to the dining room.

"I hope your trip went all right, Guy. You probably want to freshen up after the journey, but then, if you're hungry, we've got something light ready for you and a nice, long, cold beer."

The soothing effect of this greeting was immediate. Guy felt himself relax. "I am rather tired, Adie, and I'll have a shower but, yes – something to eat and drink after that would be great."

"When you're ready, Guy," was the response, "Henry and I are can fix whatever you need. And," a pause, "if you want to talk anything through, I'm here for you."

"I know you are," said Guy gratefully. "It's brilliant having you around." And he went into his bedroom, leaving his luggage for the robots to deal with.

In another part of the camp, Hod sat in his office, watching the installation of the new super-computer.

When the installing technicians had gone, it stirred into life. The voice was neither masculine nor feminine.

"Greetings, Hod. My name is Andrew. I'm so pleased we will be working together. I think I can take a lot of things off your shoulders. You really won't have to worry about anything in future. I should be able to take care of everything in due course."

SEVEN
YEARS
LATER

CHAPTER
THIRTY

The morning sun was beating down through the glass roof of the concourse at Waterloo station onto the commuters pouring off the platforms. It was rush hour, the worst time of day to travel, but Stella wanted to get down to the Isle of Wight and back in one day.

As she queued for her ticket, her thoughts turned to her mother with the usual mixture of irritation and guilt. Of course she ought to get down to see her more often, but her work was demanding and it was a question of time. And she couldn't expect Jem to come with her often. He had been very good at first, but as her mother's hold on reality had gradually slipped away, his visits had seemed increasingly pointless, as Christine now greeted him on every occasion as if it was the first time she'd met him. Conversation was always laboured anyway and tended to focus on events long past in which he had had no involvement.

With twenty minutes to wait for the Southampton train, Stella bought herself a newspaper from Smiths and a coffee and a cheese and ham croissant from a kiosk. The cheese oozed deliciously into the paper bag and she realised she was hungry.

I have to be considerate this time, she said to herself. *I mustn't be irritated with her when she gets muddled and says silly things. It's no good trying to correct her. I know it causes her distress, but I suppose I'm trying to haul her back to me and there's no point.*

Settling into her seat and revived by the hot coffee and croissant, she put these thoughts out of her mind and went through the newspaper. There was an article on the latest developments in AI which she read with interest. Camp Zebra and Kenya seemed a long way away and she had managed to avoid humanoid robots since her return to the UK, but there was no doubt that they were proliferating, as the article made clear. She had come to think that she had got the whole subject of robots completely out of proportion during that stint in Africa. It had probably been the circumstances, she reckoned: the isolation of the camp, the extreme, alien landscape and the fact that a small number of people had been cooped up together for long periods – all that had tended to increase the intensity of relationships and experiences.

I wonder what happened to Guy. Would I have fallen for him if I'd met him over here? There was no way of knowing, and anyway, Jem was the one – she was absolutely sure of that. Nevertheless, she had chosen her current role with the

NGO with a conscious determination to avoid contact with robots. The technology she used looked and felt like machines of which she was in control, and that was the way she liked it.

Looking out at the fresh May-green fields and woods of Hampshire, she wondered how she could have ever have contemplated leaving England permanently – and she had, briefly, at the peak of her enthusiasm for the desert greening project. The hedgerows were a froth of cream hedge parsley and wild cherry. Perhaps when she and Jem were ready they would move out of London. London was great for a young singleton, but not ideal for raising children. That was something she'd been thinking about a lot recently as her mid-thirties loomed. Whether Jem was thinking the same way, she couldn't be sure. It hadn't been discussed.

There was a brief panic when she reached Southampton, as the courtesy bus to the Redjet was not there and time was tight if she was not to miss her appointment with her mother's social worker. The care arrangements in place were not adequate. She had known that for some time. Her mother had become forgetful to a dangerous degree. There was a constant worry that she would leave a pan on the hob, let a stranger into the cottage or lose her keys and not be able to get back in. In fact, that had already happened, and if Christine had not been found and rescued by the local vicar who had phoned Stella, she might have come to serious harm. Having a social worker on the island who could be called by Stella in an emergency was all very well, but in between the social worker's visits Christine was vulnerable.

The simplest solution for Stella would be to install her mother in a care home – the best that could be had, naturally

– but her mother could be guaranteed to resist any such suggestion at present. Stella's mind shied away from the problem. Perhaps the social worker would come up with a solution her mother could be persuaded to accept.

The courtesy bus was full, with people standing in the aisle, but the trip to the quay was very short, and to Stella's relief, she was immediately able to join the slowly moving queue in the perspex tunnel leading to the boarding station.

Like the courtesy bus, the catamaran was full of half-term holiday-makers – many with young children, who filled the cabin with excited chatter. Stella found herself watching them with a pang. But she loved the trip across the Solent. As the waterside properties and then the narrow strips of sand which lined the estuary gave way to open sea, the island appeared tantalisingly on the horizon. The gentle coves and fertile-looking woods and fields, which had tempted the Romans to cross the water and claim it as Vectis, were looking their best on a clear, bright day like this. Cowes too looked ravishing in the sunlight, its grey stone Georgian buildings, which could appear grim in winter, had blossomed in the sunlight into softly mellow hues, and Stella's mood lifted despite her worries.

But walking up the hill in Cowes to her mother's cottage, her anxiety returned. What was she to do? It was no use expecting any help from her brother, now thousands of miles away in Canada. Even when he had been in London, he and his wife had been absorbed in their young family and had been very little help. She had the responsibility for her mother's care and that was that.

Christine's cottage was quaint but impractical, chosen at a time before her mother's dementia had taken hold and when she was still able to enjoy the walking, cycling and even sea swimming that the island offered. It seemed strange to think of that now. As she waited for the door to be answered, Stella noted the moss and slipped tiles on the roof and the peeling paint in the porch. Something would have to be done.

There were two doorbells, but her mother's deafness meant that unless she was next to where they rang she did not hear them, so the door was opened by Jane the social worker, who was clearly pleased to see Stella.

"Hello. Did you have a good journey? Thanks so much for coming," she said as she ushered Stella into the tiny hall. Before leading her through to the living room, Jane paused to say quietly, "As we discussed on the phone, we have really got to a point where things can't go on as they are."

"No, I realise that," was Stella's response. "The tricky thing is going to be to get Mum to accept any change."

"I think the dementia may actually help us there," Jane whispered. "I'm not sure how much it matters to her to be in this particular place anymore. Let's see." And she led Stella into the small living room where her mother sat in front of a coffee table furnished with teapot and cups. A large, extremely fluffy ginger cat with a flat, angry-looking face was settled comfortably on her knee.

"Hello, Mother. Don't get up, you'll disturb Cadbury." Stella bent to kiss the papery skin of the cheek and gave Cadbury a tentative stroke on the head. This caused him to half stand and raise his hind quarters to her hand, so she retreated to encourage him to resume his position.

Christine's face brightened. "Susan." She beamed.

"No, Mother, it's Stella – you know, your daughter."

A look of confusion crossed her mother's face, which then cleared as she said, "Of course, hello love. Silly me. You looked a bit like her with your back to the light."

With an effort, Stella stopped herself from responding that her aunt Susan had been dead for ten years and that, even when alive, the similarity in appearance between her and Stella had been minimal. There would also have been an age disparity of thirty years.

"Tea?" said her mother brightly, and started to get up from her seat, dislodging Cadbury, who responded with a brief squawk and strolled out of the room, tail twitching slightly.

Stella was about to tell her not to bother on her account when Jane intervened with, "That would be lovely, Christine. Do you need any help?"

"No thank you, dear," said Christine, bustling happily towards the kitchen. "You two just sit and relax."

As soon as the door closed behind her, Jane turned to Stella with a serious face. "Your mother really isn't fit to be living on her own anymore, Stella."

"I know," said Stella. "I have tried suggesting some sort of home or sheltered accommodation on the island, but she won't hear of it and I can't force her."

"Of course not – none of us can force her, and the situation is not ready for the Court of Protection yet, but something must be done. She can't go on like this. It's not safe."

"I think she might be persuaded to move closer to me in London," Stella said. "We have talked about it in the past and it would make life so much easier for me. I can't be a full-time carer, though. I have a job – an important job."

"Absolutely understood," said Jane sympathetically, "but you'll understand that just moving close to you wouldn't solve the problem on its own, even with you at the end of a phone nearby and the help of the twice-daily carer visits. She really needs someone living in now if we can't get her to go into residential care."

Stella's heart sank. "I don't think that's affordable. She's got a bit of occupational pension and her state pension, and my brother and I could top up a bit, but I've looked into it all and it wouldn't be enough."

"Well," said Jane, "I think this is where technology can help us now. Robots are starting to take over in these caring roles and they seem to be performing very well. Your mother could become one of our pioneers. How would you feel about that?"

CHAPTER
THIRTY-ONE

After a lot of searching, Stella had managed to find her mother a flat within a short bus ride of where she and Jem lived. Stella and Jem would have liked to have bought in the centre of Crouch End, near to the Clock Tower. The attraction of this small corner of London, which still retained something of the feeling of a village, was great. However, even though they both had good jobs, the centre of Crouch End was out of their price range, so they had settled on a roomy top-floor flat in a modern development in what the estate agents referred to as 'Crouch End borders', "Hornsey, really," as Stella was wont to remark drily. Nevertheless, it was still only twelve minutes' walk away from the shops, cafes and restaurants around the Clock Tower.

As Stella had expected, the sale of the Isle of Wight cottage hadn't yielded anything like enough cash to buy even a one-bedroomed flat in North London, but the interest on the proceeds of sale, her mother's pensions, and contributions from Stella and her brother were just about enough to fund the rental of a small ground-floor flat in the less-fashionable Archway and top up the cost of the care package.

Arranging the move and settling her mother in had been time-consuming and traumatic for both Stella and her mother. Uprooted from her familiar surroundings, Christine's confusion and distress had been pitiable. The situation had not been helped by the change to a London social worker and it had been essential for Stella to be present at all appointments to avoid Christine dissolving into panic.

To Stella's relief, Jem had offered to go with her to the council offices where she was to be given the details of Christine's care plan. He explained that Stella had been staying over at her mother's so much that it was as much in his interest as hers and her mother's to get things sorted out. He was missing Stella at night. *A good sign*, thought Stella.

The council offices were in a depressingly badly maintained building in one of the poorer parts of Islington. Collected from the spartan reception area by Bethany, who introduced herself as Christine's new social worker, Jem and Stella were bustled into Bethany's small office. Bethany had tried to cheer it up with a large print of Monet's garden and some jaunty mugs displayed in front of the books on the shelf along the window ledge, also a depository for dust and dead flies. They sat on uncomfortable plastic chairs and Stella tried not to adopt a defensive pose. She disliked discussing family intimacies with a stranger, but they needed the council's help with her mother, so she must get on with Bethany, who, it turned out, was to be in charge of Christine's care plan.

"You have to cooperate with all this," Jem had said to Stella before the meeting. "You can't manage this situation on your own anymore and the amount of time you're having to put in on your mother's affairs is affecting us as a couple. This has got to work."

Bethany's plump figure was shrouded in folds of multi-coloured cotton which reached almost to her ankles. Her hair was a mass of magenta frizz. From the outset Stella was irritated by her manner, which combined slightly patronising overfamiliarity with a brisk determination to get down to business, but she remained obedient to Jem's strictures. *I have to get on with this woman,* she told herself, clenching her hands together in her lap.

"Now, Stella."

Yes, you can call me that, but perhaps it would have been good to ask, thought Stella.

"We're going to take good care of Chris."

She prefers Christine, thought Stella, *but I suppose she's not in a position to stipulate anymore.*

"I've spent some time with your mum now and we've had all the reports, and I think we're all agreed, aren't we, that your mother isn't going to be able to manage on her own going forward." Stella opened her mouth to say something but failed to interrupt Bethany's flow. "It wouldn't normally be possible to provide live-in care with the resources available – that's with the support we can offer and your own contributions. So aren't we lucky, Stella, that technology has come to the rescue? Just in time; it's very new, but working very well – very well indeed. After all, we all want the best for our mums, don't we?"

"I've had the outline," said Stella as Bethany paused for breath, "but can you explain a little more how it will work? I understand that the idea is to use a robot as my mother's carer."

"That's right, Stella."

She does use my name a lot, thought Stella, but she merely said, "What sort of robot would that be?"

"Oh, the ones we use are absolutely marvellous," Bethany gushed. "Very lifelike – they really look and sound like actual people. They can do anything a carer could do. So Chris won't know the difference and it will be company for her. And they're very efficient – totally reliable. Not like – well, we have to admit, don't we, that even with the best systems, real people make mistakes and, of course..." she hesitated, "just occasionally, very, very occasionally, we get carers who aren't..." she hesitated again, "quite as caring as they might be. You'll have no worry at all when you meet the one that's been allocated to Chris."

Stella cleared her throat and offered, diffidently, "Well, I do have some direct experience of humanoid robots – in my previous job – in Africa."

"Oh, what were you doing in Africa?" Was it Stella's imagination or had Bethany's manner become a trifle less patronising?

"I'm an agronomist," said Stella. "I was involved in a project to fertilise the desert."

A note of definite respect entered Bethany's voice. This was the sort of work – not only specialist but environmentally useful – that chimed with her beliefs. "How fascinating. Did you use robots in your work?"

"We used robots a lot," said Stella. "But humanoid robots had only just been…" she hesitated, "perfected. URC, Universal Robotics Corporation, were trying them out on the personnel. I had one – two, in fact."

"Oh, that's so useful," Bethany enthused. "So you won't be nervous around them at all. They're fantastic, aren't they, and we've had such success with our dementia patients. I hate to say this, but in some ways they're better than people. I mean," she added hastily, "of course some of our carers are absolutely marvellous, but there are some jobs, well, you know, that no one likes to do – and of course we're in total control of the robots, so we don't have to worry about things like dishonesty or abuse – very rare, of course – but we have to face it, these things do happen, rarely, of course, when under the council's control. But with the robots we're in total control."

"Yes, of course." Voicing inner reservations would, Stella knew, be pointless and would only complicate the discussion.

Jem, who was aware of some of Stella's concerns, came in with, "Can you tell us a bit more about how it will work? What sort of robot will this be? I assume there will be just one?"

"Oh yes," put in Stella quickly. "Otherwise it would confuse my mother."

"Yes, yes, of course," said Bethany. "Understood. Just one. It's a male type, in this case, called Charlie. We haven't found that mixing the sexes is a problem. In fact, sometimes female clients – we like to call them clients – are reassured to have a male presence about the house. Not that they're really male, of course, we understand that. Just machines, after all. But what brilliant ones."

"Yes, indeed," responded Jem.

Stella said nothing but, "I think my mother prefers to be called 'Christine.'"

CHAPTER
THIRTY-TWO

As Jem and Stella walked back to the flat from the bus stop, Jem said thoughtfully, "I reckon it's better in general if I don't come to your mother's unless there's some DIY to be done. It confuses her if I turn up because every time she's forgotten she's met me before. Getting used to this robot is going to be hard enough."

Stella knew he was right but felt a bit disappointed with this statement. *Is it that he doesn't really see the two of us as a family?* she wondered. *He really does think of my mother as my problem, I guess.*

Moving in together had been a significant step for Stella and Jem, and for a time Stella had been content with the arrangement as it was. However, she was now thirty-four and, clichéd as it seemed, her biological clock was ticking. She would have liked to have raised the question of commitment and children, even marriage, but was afraid to do so in case it provoked a negative reaction that could damage the relationship. It might be that Jem was not ready to take on the responsibility of children, with all its life-changing potential, not to mention expense. And they would have to move to a bigger property, and she was not sure if they could afford one in the parts of North London they liked. The flat was fine for two, but there was no garden and they had had to buy a residents' permit for their one car, which was generally parked miles away from the flat as parking in Hornsey was a nightmare. *That would be a terrible pain with a pram*, thought Stella. One had to consider such things.

As they passed Lynton Road, with its picturesque Victorian terraces, Stella thought yearningly how brilliant it would be to own one. A member of her book group owned a house in the road, so she knew what they were like inside. She and Jem would be able to manage in one, even with two children. They had three bedrooms. The gardens were small, but Priory Park was four minutes away, and they would still be able to go to all the cafes, bars and restaurants they loved – not to mention, the Picture House and Arthouse cinemas. Not many places had wonderful little independent cinemas like those. But unless you had a million quid to throw at it, Crouch End was out of the question.

"Are you going over this afternoon?" Jem broke into these reflections. "I think you'd better be there when they bring this robot in."

"Yes, of course," said Stella, feeling another pang of disappointment that he was not offering to come with her.

"I don't think there'd be any chance of it working if I wasn't there. Mum hasn't a clue who Bethany is, despite the fact she's been her social worker since she arrived in London. I may stay overnight, but I'll try to get back by four tomorrow – and perhaps we can go to a film. I may need to relax. Any idea what's on?"

They had already passed the two small cinemas, so Jem said, "No worries – I'll check online from the flat and book if I think it's anything we'd like."

"Don't worry about me," was Stella's response. "Anything that's not about dementia or robots will be fine, as far as I'm concerned."

At two o'clock that day Stella found herself waiting outside her mother's flat in Junction Road, standing against the wall to avoid the passers-by who all seemed to be in a hurry and almost deafened by the roar of passing traffic.

I can't see Mum going out much here, she thought. *She'd find all this incredibly confusing and stressful. But then*, she admitted to herself, *there was no way I could have moved to be near her in the Isle of Wight – not with Jem and my job. It was perfect for her when she was well, like living in the 1950s – except in Cowes Week, of course – but I guess that's not important now. It's not really safe for her to go out on her own anymore anyway.*

After about ten minutes of waiting, she spotted Bethany walking towards her from the direction of Archway tube station. With her were two young men, walking on either side. One of them looked familiar.

"Good Lord," Stella exclaimed as they came near. "It's Hod."

And indeed, standing before her was none other than Henry O'Dwyer, older, rather fatter, but completely recognisable as the laddish technician from Camp Zebra. He seemed unsurprised to see Stella, but she decided he was just being cool. He must have been told who he was going to meet, but she couldn't believe that her name would still have meant anything to him after all this time.

As he seemed indisposed to say anything, Stella continued, "Hod, it's me, Stella, from the greening project."

Light dawned. "Stella – how're yah doin'? Great to see you. Is this your old lady we're here about?"

"Yes, I'm afraid it is," was her response, but further conversation was impossible as Bethany cut in to say brightly, "Fancy you two knowing each other." But she seemed irritated by the fact. "Before we go in, we need to have a private chat. I thought we could go to the pub across the road." Assuming consent and shepherding them across the road, she added, "They've got a little snug where we can shut ourselves away, and anyway, there's hardly anyone in at this time of day."

As they crossed, Stella said quietly to Hod, "Perhaps we can have a coffee afterwards."

"Sure thing. It'd be great to catch up," he responded, dodging traffic and following Bethany's lead into the pub.

Stella realised with a start that the other 'man' must be the robot. She didn't want to be caught studying him but stole a few looks as they went into the pub. Really the only clue to the fact that he wasn't human was his physical perfection.

Slender and well proportioned, he was a little taller than Hod. He had a full head of silky brown hair and a smooth, flawless complexion. She was sure that no passer-by would have looked at him twice, except perhaps in admiration. Only his silence was odd.

As Bethany had guessed, the pub was almost empty. The bar was a large, gloomy room, with dark wood panelling and grubby-looking etched Victorian glass. The only occupants were three solitary male drinkers nursing the dregs of pints in the darkest recesses. There was no one visible behind the bar, but a faint sound of pop music and pan clattering suggested activity in the kitchen beyond.

Bethany made no attempt to summon help at the bar but shepherded her charges through a doorway opposite which led to the promised 'snug'. It was just large enough to take a square table and bench seating. Bethany and the robot immediately took seats with their backs to the large, frosted window that took up most of the outer wall. Stella sat down opposite while Hod paused in the doorway to ask, "Wha' can I get ya' all?"

"Oh, don't bother unless someone comes," was Bethany's response. "We may not be long."

Rather taken aback and undoubtedly disappointed, Hod took a seat next to Stella but said nothing more.

"Stella," said Bethany authoritatively, "this is Charlie, and he is going to look after your mother. Isn't that so, Charlie?"

At this greeting, Charlie came to life. He stretched a hand across the table and said in the gentlest of tones, "I'm very pleased to meet you, Stella. You can be sure I'll do my very best for Christine."

Perhaps it's a bit early for you to be calling her that, thought Stella, but she merely said, "Hello Charlie," while retaining her own hand.

"Hod here is going to settle Charlie in and make sure he's in tune with all the other appliances we've installed for Christine," Bethany went on. "Since you've met Hod before, Stella, you will know that he's a robotics expert."

"Indeed," was Stella's dry response, "I couldn't have worked in the Kenyan project without being very aware of what Hod's work was all about."

Possibly picking up on some reservation in Stella's manner, Bethany went on, "It's only natural to be a little nervous of all this at first. It's very new for all of us, but as you've interacted with robots before, Stella, you'll probably find it easier than most."

"Perhaps," was the non-committal response, "but considering how difficult my mother finds it dealing with new situations and how hard it's been to settle her into the new place, I really am worried about how she's going to react when we introduce her to…" she paused, "Charlie."

Before Bethany could say anything, Charlie leaned towards Stella and fixed her with a pair of gentle-looking brown eyes. "I've been expertly programmed for the caring role, Stella. I know your mother's entire history. We'll have some wonderful times together."

"Yeah," Hod cut in, "we've put in all the stuff in the brief. He can recognise all those photos an' stuff."

"That's all the background and photos albums you gave us, Stella," said Bethany. "This isn't the first robot we've used for a dementia patient, and so far there've been no problems.

It's worked very well indeed – beyond our expectations, in fact."

"Yeah, the programming's designed by a psychologist," Hod put in, looking round to see if anyone had appeared at the bar.

"I suggest you introduce Charlie to Christine, Stella, while Hod and I go through things around the flat," Bethany went on. "We can all have a cup of tea together and then Hod and I will go and leave you to it."

"I thought I'd stay overnight for the first day as it's the weekend tomorrow," said Stella. "I was wondering how the sleeping would work, though – as there are only two bedrooms."

"I don't need a bed," said Charlie. "I'll find a place out of sight during the night, although normally I'll be in the bedroom. I don't want Christine to feel I'm in any way strange."

As there didn't seem to be any sensible response that Stella could make to this remark, she remained silent.

"Well, unless you've got questions now, Stella – and you can contact me any time with any or if you have any concerns," Bethany concluded, getting up from the table, "we'd better be getting over there and start making the introductions."

Dutifully, they all rose and followed her out, Hod casting a wistful glance behind him at the still-unmanned bar.

CHAPTER
THIRTY-THREE

Bethany and her companions had to wait some time for Stella's mother to answer the door.

"She really can't hear that doorbell," Stella remarked to Bethany.

If Bethany had detected a note of criticism in the remark, she ignored it. "Charlie is going to solve all of these little problems, Stella. Aren't you, Charlie?" She turned to the robot.

Charlie replied with a smile, "From now on I'll be answering the door, Stella. There will be no need to worry – about that, or anything."

When Christine did finally open the door, she stood for a moment in apparent confusion at the number of strangers on her doorstep, Cadbury, looking larger and fluffier than ever, wrapping himself around her ankles.

"Hello, Mum. Hello, Cadbury," said Stella, making a move towards the cat, who promptly fled into the interior of the flat.

"Hello, Mum," Stella said again, moving into the hall and depositing a firm kiss on her mother's cheek as Christine backed away. "It's me, Stella, and here's Bethany – you know, your social worker."

"Hello, dear," Christine replied, although it remained unclear as to whether she had, in reality, recognised either Stella or Bethany. As they all settled themselves in the living room, however, she at least appeared to have remembered who Stella was.

"Would you all like some tea dear?" was her first response to their presence.

"I'll get that, Mum," said Stella, making her way to the kitchen and clearing the way for Bethany to introduce Charlie.

When Stella returned with the tea tray furnished with teapot, milk jug and cups and saucers as her mother liked it, she noted that Christine had appeared to cope with her introduction to Charlie in the same vague, cheery way that she now dealt with most things – that is, unless frightened by something that she didn't understand. It was impossible to judge how much of what had been explained to her she had taken in, but it was clear that she had no memory of having met Bethany before.

At least she still knows who I am. She must have been thrown for a minute or two by all the unfamiliar people with me. It's going to be terrible when she doesn't recognise me anymore, thought Stella. *I wonder how much she has understood. It seems odd that she's so calm about a stranger moving in – and a man, at that.*

She hasn't got her hearing aid in, so she might not have heard. She often pretends she has when she hasn't, or perhaps she just hasn't registered what Bethany said.

"Charlie's going to live here with you, Mum, and look after you." Stella tried to reinforce the message. "I'll still be coming over a lot as well. It will be nice to have help with all the chores, won't it?"

The impact of this was impossible to judge. Christine merely smiled amiably and said, "Yes, that would be very nice dear."

As Stella, Bethany and Christine drank their tea, Hod and Charlie went round the other rooms in the flat, presumably checking technical compatibility issues between Charlie and other appliances, all deeply mysterious to Stella and Bethany.

At this point, Cadbury emerged from under Christine's chair and jumped onto Stella's lap. "Cadbury," she said as he circled, making himself comfortable. "I thought you'd forgotten me."

Cadbury proved a useful topic in a conversation which had been flagging, so it seemed natural on Hod and Charlie's return for Stella to introduce the cat to Charlie.

"Charlie, this is Cadbury. He's been a member of our family for many years. I hope you've been briefed about him – his food, litter etc."

"I certainly have," said Charlie, coming over and putting out a hand to stroke the cat.

Cadbury's reaction was swift and extreme. He spat loudly, lashed out and scrambled off Stella's lap, haring out of the room, his body close to the ground.

"Oh dear," Christine said in some distress. "He doesn't usually do that. He likes people."

Yes – he doesn't usually do that, thought Stella. *I hope that's not going to be a problem.*

When Bethany and Hod had gone, Stella sat with her mother in the living room drinking more tea.

Her mother had insisted on preparing this herself, despite Charlie's offer to do it. Cadbury had not reappeared. Charlie, with what appeared to be a degree of tact, kept very much in the background, disappearing, apparently to begin discreetly cleaning in the bathroom and kitchen. Stella attempted to normalise Charlie's presence to her mother by mentioning him in their conversation from time to time.

"It will be useful having Charlie here all the time, Mum. You won't have to wait for the carers to come to have your sheets changed and your meals made."

"Oh, I don't need anyone to help me do that, dear. But there is a nice lady who comes round sometimes. I think she lives next door, and it's nice to have the company."

Stella was tempted to insist that her mother register the fact that she had three different carers visiting during the day. Her mother should even have known their names by now, but she knew from experience that attempting to correct her mother only caused confusion and distress, so she merely said, "Well, Charlie will be here to help and be company all the time, so that will be even better won't it?"

"Who's Charlie, dear?" asked her mother amiably.

What's going to happen when I leave? thought Stella with a feeling of panic. *I'd better bring him in again so she sees us together before I go. Hope that will help, but I haven't a clue.*

As she went into the corridor to fetch the robot, he met her in the hall.

He smiled and placed a hand reassuringly on her arm. "I know you're nervous about leaving your mother alone with me, Stella," he said in his gentle voice, "but I am programmed to deal with this situation. Our programmers have a lot of experience of the needs of people like your mother and I know how to make her feel comfortable with having me around. It's really not safe for her to be on her own now – I think you know that, Stella. And I expect you've also picked up that a lot of the time she's lonely. I can help with that as well."

At this point, her mother called out from the living room, "Stella. Are you out there? Who are you talking to?" Stella was forced to go back into the room, followed by Charlie.

"I was just talking to Charlie, Mother."

"Who?" asked her mother, smiling.

Stella felt the customary irritation creeping back into her voice and tried to repress it. "You know, Mum, Charlie, your new friend who's going to be here to look after you."

"Oh, yes dear," said her mother vaguely, and looked expectantly at Charlie as he took a seat opposite Stella.

He smiled and said, "I've just been doing a bit of clearing up, Christine. I wonder if you'd like some more tea."

"No more for me, thank you dear," was the response. And after a pause, "Nice to meet you. Have you and Stella been going out long?"

"Charlie's not my boyfriend," said Stella carefully. "He's your new carer. You know, Bethany, your social worker, brought him."

"Oh, I don't need a carer dear," said her mother emphatically.

At this point, Charlie took over. "Shall we look at the photo album, Christine? I can see it over there."

Christine perked up immediately. "Oh, yes. I can show you where we used to live. Such a shame we had to leave it for Ted's work. He likes it here now, though."

"Dad's dead now, Mum," Stella couldn't resist saying, but Charlie spoke over her, so she wasn't sure her mother had heard.

"Oh yes," Charlie said, taking the album from the bookcase and moving his chair to be next to Christine. "I think I've found the photo. I expect Stella has to get back to work, so we'll say goodbye shall we? She's seen all these before."

I can take a hint, thought Stella, *and it's true that there seems to be nothing else that I can do here.*

She got up, pushing her chair back against the wall, and went over to kiss her mother's papery cheek.

"Yes, Mum. Better be going. I'll pop in again tomorrow."

"All right, dear," her mother responded, although she was already looking at the album pages Charlie was presenting to her.

"Thank you for coming. Oh, look – there's the house and there's Ted. Such a handsome man – still is, of course."

As she left, Stella could just hear Charlie's soothing response. "He certainly is handsome, Christine. And what a lovely garden that is."

CHAPTER
THIRTY-FOUR

Instead of the promised coffee, Stella and Hod had agreed to meet the following weekend in Crouch End. In the end Stella decided to take Jem along, partly to avoid any misunderstanding on Hod's part, and partly to increase Jem's involvement in the situation. Anyway, she thought they would get on, although they were very different.

It was a still, warm evening and the shrubs planted along the borders in front of the ground-floor flats on their estate were in full creamy flower, giving off a strong, slightly sour smell rather like privet. The trees along the banks of the canal which ran alongside the railway line and opposite the flat were in fresh green leaf, and the rainy April had replenished the lawns, which were attracting some of the young mothers from the social housing on the lower slopes of the development.

They were sitting on blankets gossiping, keeping half an eye on prams containing sleeping babies and toddlers trying out their walking unsteadily on the grass.

Africa seemed a long away and Stella thought, as she had many times since her return to the UK, how happy she was to be back. It felt like home. It felt safe.

"How do you know this guy again?" asked Jem, although Stella thought she had explained. "I mean, I know he's a tech guy and he was out in Africa, but it sounds as if you knew him quite well."

Jem was well aware that Stella had had a romantic interlude in Kenya with someone called Guy Trenhaile – a subject covered briefly and not returned to on either side, but Stella thought the question was probably not as casual as it sounded. *He's trying to find out if there was anything between me and Hod.*

She laughed. "If you're wondering if anything went on with him, you can stop. Hod is definitely not my type. You'll be able to tell that when you meet him."

"I'm not sure I know what your type is," said Jem disingenuously.

"You're my type," said Stella. "Don't fish." And she linked arms with him, giving him a peck on the cheek. "There were only a few hundred people out there in the camp, and not many of them were under forty, so I got to know most of the younger ones quite well. We all used to meet up in the bar at night. There wasn't much else to do when we were back at camp. When they gave me the robots to try out, it was good to have Hod to bounce questions off – him being an expert and all that. Not that he was very sympathetic to my worries about them."

"Never really got to the bottom of your worries," Jem said, turning to look at her. "I would have thought it was quite an interesting thing to be involved in. I know these things are being used quite a lot now, but at the time it must have been incredibly exciting."

"It's hard to explain," she said. "A few worrying things happened – one of the wives had a nervous breakdown after getting one and when her husband got one he destroyed it and then committed suicide."

"Good God!" Jem exclaimed. "If they thought those things were caused by the robots, surely the company wouldn't have rolled them out like they have."

"The thinking was that these were vulnerable people who cracked under the strain of being in the middle of nowhere in Africa. I know that's what Hod thinks. As far as he's concerned, the robots are just very high-tech machines and totally under control. And…" she paused, "a lot of the people who tried them out really liked them." *Guy Trenhaile, for one,* she thought.

"Well, you know," said Jem. "The crack-up theory does make sense. Cooped up in the middle of the desert – not much to do to relax. Wouldn't fancy it myself." Jem was a lawyer and a city boy to his fingertips.

"Look, I know that this robot solves a problem with my mother," Stella went on, "but I didn't feel comfortable myself having the things around the house – and not just that, there were other sorts of robots and AI everywhere. It all got a bit much."

For some reason, she didn't want to go into the experience out at the pods. "I'm glad I've met up with Hod. Hopefully he can calm me down about it. I do want this to work you know. We can keep in touch quite easily 'cos he's living in Kilburn. I ought to warn you – he's a bit laddish, though."

"I can do laddish." Jem laughed.

Not really, thought Stella. *That's one of the things I love about you.*

Stella and Jem's favourite tapas bar was near the Clock Tower, a few yards into Middle Lane which ran parallel to what was in effect the high street of Crouch End. Small and low-ceilinged, the bar's white-washed walls hung with bright Spanish posters and the back door, this evening open to a small walled courtyard, managed to give it a reasonably Mediterranean feel. This was enhanced by the darkly exotic-looking staff, who spoke with charming foreign accents. The fact that on closer acquaintance they turned out to be Romanian rather than Spanish did not in any way damage the ambiance. It was an extremely popular spot with the young professionals and media people who now bought up all the period property that came on the market in the locality.

Hod was already there when they arrived, having settled himself with a long beer at a table by the door. He had obviously seen them coming as he was on his feet as they came in, his transatlantic tones ringing out above the animated weekend chatter behind him.

"*Stella* – hi. Great to see yah. And this must be Jem. Whadya having?"

Having clapped Jem on the back, he resumed his seat and looked round for a waitress, who appeared promptly with Eastern European efficiency.

"Lovely to see you Hod," said Stella.

"Nice to meet you," from Jem. "I've heard a lot about you."

Something of an exaggeration, that, thought Stella but said nothing, and Hod let the remark pass.

"So then, Hod," Stella went on as they took their seats with their backs to the window. "What do you think of Crouch End?"

"Yeah, looks cool," was the response, "but I'm pretty happy in Kilburn. Can't believe the prices back here, though. Good thing I managed to save quite a bit back in Africa."

"Yes, when we bought," said Stella, "we could only afford Crouch End borders – Hornsey, really – and we've both got reasonable incomes, although now I work for an NGO mine's nothing like as good as Jem's. But it's nice, and we can still walk into the cinemas and bars. About twelve minutes, we reckon."

"Cinemas, plural – in a little place like this?" Hod was genuinely surprised.

"They're independents – small arthouse efforts," explained Jem. "You'd be less surprised if you knew the resident profile around here. Lots of custom for art with a capital 'A.'"

"Not buying at the moment," said Hod. "Not totally sure what my plans are. May try the States for a bit later on."

Yes, thought Stella, *none of the tech guys wanted to commit for the long term. All on contracts. All just passing through.*

The drinks arrived as Stella and Hod caught up with what they had been doing for the past seven years. Stella's return to the UK had been pretty straightforward. Hod had hopped around a bit with URC, mostly in Africa but more recently in Spain.

"Really dug Spain," he said. "Barcelona is my kinda town. 3am in the Ramblas – unbeatable. Like Piccadilly Circus at midday, only better – warmer, for one thing," he added thoughtfully.

"Always did wonder how you guys could drink until the early hours and be up doing your jobs the next day," said Stella.

"Well, to be fair, we don't do normal office hours. Like to start late and end late, and if ya end late, ya need to unwind before shut-down."

He means going to bed, of course, thought Stella with amusement, *but what an appropriate phrase to use in the circumstances. They really are a different breed.*

"So you're still with Universal Robotics?" Jem had rejoined the table and the conversation, having been to the toilets in the garden and then stopped to chat to an acquaintance on the way back.

"Contract only," replied Hod, confirming Stella's guess. "Did a coupla stints for other outfits, but URC pay well and they're definitely at the top of the game for humanoid robots, which is ma main thing. Was a bit worried back there in Kenya when they brought in a new super job which could do the programming, but it was just about adapting the way I worked and getting used to some newer technology. Can't do without the human element. That's why URC are so great – always upfront with the technology. That's given me a step up the ladder."

"There suddenly seem to be quite a few of these humanoid robots about," Jem said. "I was at a client's in the City recently and they had one on reception. Pretty spectacular blonde too – and massively efficient – better than the real thing they had before. But Stella says she didn't really get on with them out in Kenya."

"We've refined them a bit since then, but they were pretty good models. Tried to get it into Stella here's head that they're just appliances – like her laptop, only much, much more complicated – but don' think I convinced her." And he looked questioningly at Stella.

"I'm probably being irrational," she said, "but I find it hard to believe that you guys at HQ are in total control. They seem so lifelike – and…" she hesitated, "when I had two of them in the house, I sometimes felt that they were communicating with each other without saying anything. Even sometimes that they knew what I was thinking."

"Nah." If Hod had heard such concerns expressed by anyone else he gave no indication of it. "They *could* communicate between themselves without speaking if we programmed 'em to do it, but we didn't for that experiment. Wanted 'em to seem completely lifelike. If they're working in teams on the same project, though, it's a smart thing to do. I've enabled non-verbal communication between Charlie and some of the computerised stuff in your ma's apartment, Stella – just so you know. Things like the cleanbot may seem to have lives of their own, but it's just Charlie controlling them – an', a' course, we're controlling Charlie."

"So it's possible to have a situation where a lot of robots and other things controlled by AI are all hooked into some sort of central computer in a remote control room?" Jem seemed fascinated by the idea.

"Yeah – that's right. All done remotely. Only a matter of time until everything in the country is connected up – computers, phones, electricity supplies, cars, robots. Ace!"

"Are you saying they could all be controlled by the sort of big computer you worked with in Camp Zebra?" said Stella. "What happens if that goes wrong? That sounds like a recipe for disaster." Her voice rose on the last word.

"But that's wha' we're there for." Hod laughed. "Ultimately it's the tech guys in control of the main computers. An' we're *definitely* human."

"No offence, Hod," said Jem jovially, "but I'm not sure I find the idea of everything being under the control of a group of tech guys totally reassuring."

He and Hod laughed at this. Stella tried a smile.

CHAPTER
THIRTY-FIVE

May turned into flaming June, and Stella and Jem found themselves frequently making use of a special benefit enjoyed by the four top-floor flats in their block. All the flats on the estate had balconies, and in theory the large flat roof, which took up half of the top floor, was a common area available to all flats in the block. Like many communal spaces, however, it was in practice only used by those with direct access to it – in this case the four penthouse flats grouped along one side behind a glassed-in corridor of which Stella and Jem's flat was one.

Stella and Jem had bought a wooden garden table and benches, and had, with some difficulty, taken them up to the roof for their own use in the small lift. Even if they didn't eat out there, they liked to take a bottle of wine out and sit watching the sun go down behind the grand Victorian structure perched on its hill, known affectionately to all locals as 'Ally Pally'.

On one particularly still evening very near the solstice, Stella had left work early to stop off in Crouch End and buy the ingredients for a special supper.

One of her colleagues had given her his recipe for a dish called 'tavas', a local dish from the district of Greece where he had been brought up.

The butcher chatted as he obligingly cut the lamb into five-centimetre squares as requested. "What are you making?" he asked, expertly wielding his enormous knife and using it and his hand to push the squares created to the side of the marble slab it rested on.

Stella loved the fact that some of the shopkeepers now recognised her and would make friendly conversation when she went in. "It's called 'tavas,'" she replied. "You probably know it. It's baked with yogurt, rice, nutmeg and garlic – egg as well."

"Not one that I know," he replied. "Sounds a bit like the Turkish iskender kebab."

"I wanted to make a special meal tonight," Stella said, "and I've had iskender in Turkish restaurants and really love it, so I'm hoping this will be delicious." She remembered now that the butcher was Cypriot whereas her colleague came from mainland Greece. *Perhaps that makes a difference,* she thought. *Regional dishes, like Yorkshire pudding.*

"Here you are, young lady," the butcher said, smiling amiably and twisting the corners of the plastic bag into which he had decanted the lamb. "If it's for a man – he's a lucky guy," he said, handing her the package and smiling as he would for any pretty young woman.

Having stopped at the greengrocer for salad and returned to the clock tower to buy a special bottle of Rioja to go with the tavas, Stella set off along Tottenham Lane for the flat. Her bag was quite heavy now and she could have caught the bus for the short distance to Hornsey High Street, but it was such a lovely, balmy evening that she decided to walk. People were sitting by summer-opening doors all along the narrow pavement, enjoying the early-evening sunshine and chatting or reading their *Evening Standard*.

She was just passing the glass frontage of the Picture House when her mobile rang. She put her carrier bag down and had to take off her backpack to answer the phone which was stowed safely in an inside pocket. She felt a slight irritation, as she assumed it was Jem calling. *Why can't he wait until he gets home? I hope he's not going to be late*, she said to herself.

But it wasn't Jem; it was Charlie.

It was not one of Stella's days for visiting her mother. She had now reduced her visits to her mother to twice a week and she had developed the habit of calling in for about twenty minutes on her way home. In the first week of Charlie's stay, she had visited every day before feeling sufficiently assured that her mother had accepted, indeed welcomed, Charlie's presence and ministrations to feel comfortable about reducing them. Indeed, she had increasingly come to feel that her mother, although apparently pleased to see her on arrival, was also slightly relieved when she left. Certainly conversation between them tended to be laboured, limited as it was to Stella asking her mother what she had done that day – a question which Christine usually referred to Charlie for an answer. Stella's attempts to interest her mother in her own day at work were met with such vagueness and obvious incomprehension that she had increasingly felt it a waste of time. She had persisted, though, really for want of anything else to say. She was determined to keep up her regular visits though, despite the fact that it meant she got home about two hours later, which came to seem a chore and certainly interfered with the routine she and Jem had established for their evenings. It was very important to make sure that all was well with the set-up – and that the 'Charlie thing' was working.

"Stella," Charlie's voice came through her phone with remarkable clarity, considering its softness. "There's really nothing to worry about but I did want to let you know that your mother had a slight episode today. She's completely recovered now, but she became very faint and confused for a time, and I thought I ought to let you know. I've made a note in the log."

"Oh no." She pushed the carrier bag and rucksack against the wall so as not to block the pavement and turned away from the street to try to shut out the traffic noise. "What is it? Should we get the doctor out?"

"I think we can expect these little incidents from time to time now Stella. They're not strokes – just little periods when the blood flow to the brain is interrupted briefly."

"I wasn't told we could expect anything like this," said Stella with a combination of alarm and irritation. *How come a robot could know more about her mother's health than she did?*

"Oh, yes – it's there in her records, Stella. The doctor probably didn't want to worry you unnecessarily – and I was concerned about that, but I thought it was important that you should know. It's essential that you have complete confidence in me, Stella. Looking after someone's mother is a great responsibility and I want you to feel that I will always put your mother's wellbeing first."

Stella now had one finger in her ear so that she could focus better on what was being said on the phone. "I think I'd better come round right now, Charlie. Neither of us is a doctor, and anyway, it might develop into something really serious."

"I really don't think that's a very good idea, Stella. Christine is in bed now. She's quite comfortable, and she might be confused and alarmed if you suddenly turned up after she'd gone to bed. Of course I'm not a medical expert, but I am familiar with all the details of your mother's health and I can get advice the moment I need it – or take your mother to hospital if there was an emergency. The Whittington is just up the hill."

"Please don't worry anymore. I would let you know immediately if there were any serious developments. You go ahead and enjoy the sunshine on your lovely roof terrace. And please be assured, I will take the best care of your mother. I'll always put her wellbeing first."

"Have a lovely evening. Goodbye now."

I guess I can't go now he's said that, Stella said to herself, thinking also, if truth be told, of the special meal with Jem that she had planned. As she picked up her bags and carried on walking a further thought came to her. *I don't remember saying anything to Charlie about a roof terrace.*

Later, on the roof with Jem, the empty plates and half-consumed bottle of wine on the table between them, Stella couldn't help returning to the phone call, even though she had blurted the whole thing out as soon as Jem had come through the door after work.

"It's not right that this… this machine, knows more about my mother's health than I do. And what did he mean about getting advice? Surely no one at the surgery would speak to someone who wasn't a relative."

"Perhaps he meant from another robot," said Jem tentatively, realising that this might not be an idea that would have appeal to Stella.

"Oh my God." She pushed away her plate and turned aside from the table. "I can't believe I'm dealing with this sort of thing again. I really don't think I can stand it."

Jem brought his chair round to sit next to her and took her hands in his. "You know, love, you're going to have to get used to these androids or whatever they're called. They are coming in everywhere. They've got one at one of the windows in the bank now – just for routine transactions, but if you go online they're everywhere in advertisements, giving advice. The truth is that Charlie has solved a huge problem – not just for you, but for us. If we're going to spend our lives together, that is."

There were not many statements Jem could have made to distract her from her concern about Charlie and the advance of the robots, but this was one of them.

"Do you see us as being together for the long term then?" she asked, hardly daring to hope.

"Now, do you think I'd have agreed to buy a flat with you if I didn't?" said Jem, putting his arms round her. "That was a big commitment as far as I was concerned, but now I'm ready for a bigger one. How about you?"

He fished in his pocket and brought out a small box. "This seems like as good a time as any. Will you marry me?"

"I think I've always known you were the right one," she said as she opened the box to find a square-cut diamond nestling in a mound of dark blue velvet.

"Oh," she exclaimed in surprised delight, "it's like the one I saw in that window in Ireland."

"More than that," said Jem, "it *is* the one you saw in Ireland. I went back the next day and got it while you were having your hair cut."

"I don't… I don't know what to say. I'm so happy." Stella had to put the box down to wipe away tears and blow her nose.

"That's a funny way of showing it, you dear, silly old thing," said Jem, taking her in his arms and stroking the hair back from her face. "We've got a lot to talk about, but for this evening shall we just sit here, enjoy the sunset on our little terrace – well, I know it's not ours, but no one else seems to use it – and be happy together?"

"Oh Jem," Stella whispered, "I do love you." And just for the moment, any thoughts about her mother, Charlie and robots in general were far from her mind.

CHAPTER
THIRTY-SIX

One of the things Stella liked best about the flat was the way that on sunny mornings the light came streaming onto the bed through the slatted blinds of the large, east-facing bedroom window. *I shall miss this*, she thought as she lay next to Jem the following Saturday. *That is, if we have a house or a ground-floor flat where we don't get as much sun because we have trees or things outside the window. Of course, it would be nice to have a garden – and we'll need one if…* She hesitated to allow herself to think about children. They hadn't been mentioned yet – in fact, there hadn't yet been a discussion about a wedding date – but she thought the children thing was a discussion she and Jem would have to have before they got married.

"Not all men want children," her mother had once said to her. "Not all women either. You should remember when you come to get married. It's important to get these things straight between the two of you before you commit yourselves. Your father never really wanted children. It was you and Patrick coming along which finished us off as a couple. You might as well know the truth."

Stella had been two when her biological father had left and four when her mother had remarried the only man Stella had consciously thought of as her father. She had nothing but fond memories of Ted, her stepfather, who had died shortly after her return from Africa – a quiet, kindly man who had given the family financial security and made her mother happy.

Stella hardly ever thought of her real father. She had talked to Patrick about him occasionally, but Patrick, who had been four when he left, claimed he had no more memory of him than she did and was profoundly uninterested in discussing, or even, it seemed, thinking about him. Now, with the possibility of having her own children with Jem before her, Stella found herself wondering what her father had really been like (or was like now – she had no idea whether he was alive or dead). She was a scientist and only too well aware of the implications of genetics. *I could try asking my mother,* she thought. *She would never talk about him when we were younger, but now she sometimes seems to think she's still married to him. She appears to have forgotten Ted completely. I could try asking her. If I could get to her stash of photos, there may be some of my father that's she's forgotten to get rid of. I'll try next time I'm round there.*

Jem began to stir beside her and she rolled over to kiss him.

"Mmm." He stretched and then yawned. "That's nice."

"I'll get the coffee." Stella bounded out of bed and opened the blinds. It looked warm outside already, so she slid back the French window and, having wrapped her robe around her, stepped out onto the balcony, letting the slats fall back behind her to shield Jem, who was naked, from public view. *Not that I would think anyone could see us up here*, she thought.

Beyond the trees and the canal, the roofs and towers of central London were sparkling in the morning sun. Life seemed full of possibilities and she was conscious of a feeling of absolute contentment.

"Are you going round to see your mother today?" Jem asked from inside the bedroom.

His voice sounded as if he had got up, so Stella went back inside. "Sorry," she said, "I really am going to make the coffee. It's just that it was such a lovely morning I had to pop outside to have a look." And she squeezed past Jem, who was pulling on some jogging pants, to cross the hall to the galley kitchen.

"Yes," she said after a pause, against the background of the boiling kettle. "I was going to make it tomorrow, but in view of that phone call from Charlie last night I think it ought to be today."

"I'm sure everything's OK," said Jem, "but I know you'll be worrying if you don't go and check the situation out yourself, so it's better if you do. I can do the shopping while you're there – and I'm going to the gym after we've had our coffee, so we could meet up again in Crouch End for a late lunch if you fancy. How about Florian's?"

"I'd love that," said Stella. "You're right – I'd better go today. I'm not going to let Charlie know in advance, though

– although I sometimes think he knows anyway. He never seems surprised when I turn up, whether I've told him or not."

"Why would he seem surprised?" said Jem from the bathroom. "He's only a machine."

CHAPTER
THIRTY-SEVEN

Charlie answered the door to Stella on the first ring – almost as if he had been standing behind it when she rang.

"Come in, Stella," he said, standing back to let her pass. "Your mother is having a very good day today. We have been looking at the old photographs again. You might want to look at some of them with Christine. It would be good for you both to share some memories."

Stella paused in the hall, forcing Charlie to pause too before they both joined her mother in the living room. "I couldn't help being terribly worried about your call last night, Charlie. Obviously I've known for a long time that Mum had some problems with her arteries and her blood pressure, but I thought her medication had it all under control."

"I am completely on top of your mother's medical conditions, Stella. I have been given all the information I need to deal with them and I do make sure that she takes her medication regularly. If anything unexpected happens, I can access immediate medical advice on how to deal with it."

"From the GP, you mean?" asked Stella. "Well, I've never managed to get hold of anyone from our practice out of hours – it's always some locum."

"Not that way, Stella. All carers have an app which enables them to tap into the best source of advice. Now the records are all centrally kept it's a great help."

Does he mean he's getting advice from another machine? wondered Stella. She almost felt it would be rude to question Charlie further. *I'll ask Hod – he'll tell me*, she thought as she led the way into the living room.

As Charlie had suggested, her mother was sitting at the table with photograph albums and single photos spread around her. She greeted Stella with pleasure, although Stella noted that she didn't use her name.

"Shall we all look at these together?" said Charlie, pulling up another chair so that he and Stella could sit on either side of Christine.

"I don't know who that is," said Christine, pushing away a photograph of herself and Stella's stepfather.

"That's Ted, Mum, Dad, my stepfather – your husband."

"Stepfather?" Christine looked at Stella with confusion. "Don't be silly, dear," she said, sounding almost angry. "Don't talk nonsense – *that's* your father." And she pointed to a photograph that Stella had never seen before. It was of her mother in a long, white wedding dress standing next to a tall young man in whom Stella could see some resemblance to Patrick.

"Is that David, Mum?" said Stella, trying to keep her voice steady. "Is that my real dad?"

"Of course that's your father," her mother responded sharply, and then, with a change of mood, "That's enough. I don't know who a lot of these people are. I'm going to get rid of them, cluttering up the place."

"Don't do that," said Stella in panic, trying to move the albums and photographs away from her mother, who seemed intent on sweeping them to the floor.

"That's all right, Christine." Charlie's calm tones cut in. "I'll put them away for you."

"No," said Christine shrilly. "No, I want to get *rid* of them."

"Of course, of course," he responded soothingly, gathering them expertly together and gliding out of the room.

Stella, feeling upset and shaken, moved away from the table and attempted to calm the mood. "Shall we have a coffee, Mum?" she suggested, more for something to say than for any other reason.

Her mother appeared to have calmed down but was left with an air of bemusement. She remained sitting facing the table, clearly confused as to what had led her to sit there.

"Come and sit over here, Mum," said Stella, getting up to lead Christine to her customary chair. "And I'll get us some coffee."

"That's all right, Stella." Charlie had reappeared and was standing in the doorway. "I'll get the coffee. You have some time with your mother – and…" he paused, "don't worry about those things."

He means the photos, I suppose, thought Stella. *Has he guessed how important some of them are to me? I suppose it's obvious, really. Still, how strange that they had them out just when I was coming. I wonder how much he knows about me as well as my mother.*

Once the photographs had been removed, much to Stella's relief, Christine's normal air of cheery vagueness reasserted itself. They were able to sit over the coffee and biscuits provided by Charlie, for the remainder of Stella's visit making desultory conversation. Finally, having exhausted both the subject of her week at work and Jem's proposal of marriage, both of which were met with a degree of sunny incomprehension, Stella got up to leave.

"Goodbye dear." Her mother raised her cheek to be kissed.

Of course I'm glad she doesn't mind my going, said Stella to herself, *but it does make me feel a bit superfluous – and a bit sad.*

She was met in the hall by Charlie, who handed her a heavy carrier bag. "I think the time has come for you to take these, Stella," he said, and she saw that he had packed all the albums and loose photographs that they had been looking at.

"Oh, surely they're my mother's," said Stella, startled.

"It's often the case that people at a certain stage of dementia destroy photographs, Stella, because they can find the fact that they don't recognise the people in them anymore frightening. I think we are getting to that stage with Christine, aren't we? And some of these photographs are of great importance to you, I believe, Stella."

Stella was still trying to decide on the implications of that remark as she sat on the bus back to Crouch End, the carrier bag full of photos on the seat beside her.

CHAPTER
THIRTY-EIGHT

Florian's restaurant had a small, unobtrusive frontage in Middle Lane three minutes' walk from the Clock Tower. Once one went in, however, it opened out like a TARDIS, revealing a sunny rear room and patio. Stella found Jem seated outside with a newspaper and a bottle of Peroni.

"Hello, love – how did it go?" He got up to kiss her and pull out a chair opposite his.

"Mum seemed fine," said Stella, "but I can't help it, I find Charlie spooky. Mum doesn't, of course. One depressing thing – she wanted to throw away all the family photos. Charlie says it's not unusual for people with dementia to do that."

"Well," said Jem gently, "he's probably been programmed with the results of a lot of research into the subject. He's a computer after all. If you'd googled and come up with that information, you wouldn't find it spooky."

"I suppose that's true," said Stella. "But it's not just that. He seems to know all about Mum's medical records. I didn't know she had narrowed arteries. And really, this is *very* spooky: I sometimes think he knows what I'm thinking."

"Ah – as far as the medical records are concerned, as they're all held on computer, wouldn't it be likely that Charlie's been linked in to them? That doesn't seem sinister to me. On reading your mind, though, I have to say, love," he reached over and put his hand over hers on the table, "I think you're getting things a bit out of proportion there. Hod's explained it all to you – why can't you rely on him? He's the expert."

"I suppose you're right," Stella said grudgingly, but she found she couldn't stop thinking about it even as they ordered their lunch.

When the waitress had gone, she said suddenly, "I'm just going to pop out and phone Hod. Sorry – I know it's a pain, but I can't stop thinking about it."

"OK," Jem said resignedly, "if it'll put your mind at rest. You've probably got at least ten minutes before the pasta arrives, but then could we please relax and enjoy our lunch in the sunshine? After all, we're celebrating aren't we?"

"Of course," said Stella, leaning over to give him a peck on the cheek. "Sorry to be a pain," she repeated.

Taking her phone out, Stella went back into the street and looked around for a quiet spot. In the end she tucked herself into the doorway of an empty shop just along the road from Florian's and out of earshot of the chatter from the restaurant garden. She dialled Hod's mobile. *It's 1.30 – he should be up by now*, she thought.

Hod was up, or certainly awake, and he answered immediately in the manner which had become familiar in Camp Zebra. "Hod here."

"Oh, Hod." Stella's voice was apologetic. "I'm really sorry to bother you about this."

"Stella," was the amiable and expansive reply, "no problem. Great to hear from you. Just thinking last night we should get together again – really dug that tapas place."

"That would be lovely, Hod – any weekday evening really. Weekends are a bit tied up with one thing and another." She hesitated but ploughed on. "I hope you don't mind if I pick your brains again about robots – well, about Charlie in particular."

"C'mon, Stella – you're not still worrying about that stuff?"

"Well, I am a bit – but perhaps you can clear a few things up that would stop it."

"Shoot," said Hod. "Anything you like – apart from state secrets." He laughed.

"Well," said Stella. "He seems to know all about my mother's medical history. Is that right? Is that OK?"

"Sure. When we put these bots in as carers they have direct access to the NHS computer – and to really fast medical advice."

"Where would that come from?" asked Stella.

"From the diagnostic and treatment function," Hod replied. "Look, I know what you're thinking, but this stuff is all programmed in and checked by medical experts – human ones. Those computers have access to research from all over the world."

Yes, thought Stella, *I suppose I knew the answer to that, really, so I'll just have to live with it.*

"But there's something else," she went on. "Is there any possibility that, well, that Charlie would be able to read my mind? Sorry if I've asked you that before."

Hod seemed to take this question a bit more seriously than the previous one, but his reply was adamant. "Look, these are fantastic machines. They have a lot in their programmes about human psychology. But as for reading minds? No – no way. The technology's not there, and even if it were we wouldn't let it be used. You can get that right out of your head, hun."

CHAPTER
THIRTY-NINE

Stella arrived at the table at the same time as the orecchiette with sausage ragu.

"I could eat this every day," said Jem, making enthusiastic use of the pepper mill.

"It's a bit fattening to have every day," sighed Stella, "but I really can't resist it when I come here. Yes, please," she said, holding her glass out for some of the Nero d'Avola, which was sitting, opened, on the table.

Jem poured Stella a glass and then, raising his own, which was already half empty, "Here's to us, my love."

Stella raised her own glass and clinked with his, smiling.

"You look a bit more cheerful," he said. "How was Hod?"

"Hod is fine." Stella smiled. "And he wanted to come back to Bar Esteban so I said we'd meet him there after work on Wednesday – about seven o'clock."

"I might be a bit late," said Jem. "There's a departmental meeting starting at four – they can go on a bit, but I'll see you both there. He's great – very entertaining. Did he manage to reassure you?"

"I suppose so." Stella looked thoughtfully at her glass. "Actually he said more or less what you did. That Charlie has access to the NHS computer and diagnostic tools and that – no, he's definitely not reading my mind. Though he did say they have some sort of programming in 'human psychology'. So I guess that's how Charlie intuited that I'd be interested in the photos – and especially of my real father. I never knew him of course. He left just after I was born. I know Charlie was programmed with the family history, so I suppose it follows."

"There you are then," said Jem, leaning over to give her cheek a quick pat. "You've answered your own question."

"I suppose I do owe him a debt of thanks," Stella went on between mouthfuls, "because it looks as though Mum was about to get rid of all the family photos, in which case I'd never have known what my real father looked like."

She put down her fork, brought the carrier bag up from under the table and fished around until she brought out a small photo. "This is him," she said.

Jem took the photo and looked at it for several minutes while continuing to fork pasta into his mouth. "He looks like your brother," he said finally. "It must be strange to know what he looks like after all this time. Or I should say *looked* like."

"Yes." Stella took the photograph back and replaced it in the carrier bag, taking care not to bend it in the process. "I suppose I'll never know what he looks like now. Whether he has another family. Whether he's alive or dead."

Jem took her spare hand again and held it firmly. "It's a shame," he said, "but we're going to make our own family. And I won't be going anywhere – promise."

The following day found Stella and Jem pouring over Stella's family photos which were spread out on the dining table. Stella could find no more of her father.

"That's Ted," she said, pushing a series of holiday snaps over to Jem. They showed Stella and her brother as children and adolescents in various holiday locations, usually in a family group with a highly recognisable Christine and an amiable-looking middle-aged man. "He was a real sweetie. I'm so sorry you didn't get to meet him. No children of his own, he always treated Pat and me as if we were his. We called him 'Dad' – he adopted us legally. And," she added thoughtfully, "I'm so sorry he won't be around to take me up the aisle. There's no reason these days why a mother can't do it, but I'm not sure Mum would be up to it."

Jem was slow to respond to this remark, and Stella experienced a spasm of nerves. *We haven't talked dates yet. Perhaps he thinks the proposal's enough for the time being. And I suppose it should be – but I'm thirty four and my mother won't be around for ever.*

Perhaps to distract attention from the implications of Stella's remark, or perhaps from genuine curiosity, Jem handed a photograph to Stella, saying, "Who is this? She looks a bit like your mother but taller and thinner."

"Oh, yes," Stella said, taking the photo from him. "That's my Aunt Sarah. You haven't met her yet. She lives in Scotland now, so we don't see her very often, but I would like you to meet. I think she and my mother had a bit of a falling-out a few years ago – I'm not sure what it was about, but since then I've only seen her about twice when she came down for my cousin's wedding – he lives in London – and then to help with his baby last year. I'm also not sure how much she knows about Mum's dementia. She hadn't visited her on the Isle of Wight for years, so I think for some time it's just been Christmas and birthday cards. I like her, though. She's a pretty gutsy lady – widowed a few years ago and very independent."

"It would be good to meet her," said Jem, leaning back from the table. "You can't meet my parents, of course, I'm sorry about that, but I have loads of other relatives I want to introduce you to. Is that cousin you mentioned your only one? I've got loads."

"Yes," said Stella, "Bob's my only cousin. Here's a photo. We used to get on really well when we were kids. I haven't seen him for ages either. We'll have to have him and his wife over sometime. I only met her a few times, but she seemed nice. Sunday lunch would be best so they can bring Rosie – otherwise they'd have to get a babysitter."

"I'd like that," Jem said, "but perhaps we should take them to a pub with a garden. This flat isn't ideal for small kids – or kids at all, if it comes to that."

No – that's very true, thought Stella, but she only said, "Yes, let's do that."

"I suppose your cousin could give you away – when we get to that stage," offered Jem. "Shall we put these away now and get some lunch – I suppose it's brunch really? I bought some muffins for eggs benedict if you're up for it."

"Certainly am," said Stella, stowing the photographs away in a box file. "You do the eggs – I'll do the coffee. I still haven't got the hang of poaching them in boiling water."

"Sorry," said Jem. "That poacher had to go. I'll show you again sometime, but today I'm too hungry to slow down for a training session."

As it was a warm, sunny spring day, they ate their eggs benedict on the balcony looking over the freshly green treetops at the moorhens and ducks on the canal.

"You know, what we were talking about got me thinking," said Stella. "My father could still be alive. There are ways of tracing people, aren't there? How do you go about it?"

"Well, if I were you," said Jem, "I'd start with your aunt. Even if your mother banished him from your life, it doesn't mean your aunt did. She might at least know where he went after he left, which would be a start. And she could probably tell you something about the break-up – what happened back then."

"Wow – that's a brilliant idea. I guess I never asked her anything before because I didn't want to put her in a difficult position with my mother, but that doesn't really come into it anymore. I'm going to phone her tonight. She lives in Edinburgh by the way."

CHAPTER
FORTY

The train journey from London Kings Cross to Edinburgh Waverley takes four and a half hours and passes through some spectacular landscapes. Stella had not visited her aunt in Edinburgh since the funeral of her uncle two years earlier, so she had booked a couple of days' leave which she intended to add to the weekend so that she could spend some time reconnecting with her aunt and enjoying Edinburgh. Her aunt had been delighted with the call.

"Come for as long as you want, Stella. It's been too long."

So just a week after the discussion with Jem about tracing her father, Stella found herself in the silent carriage on the way to Edinburgh. She wanted to shut out distractions so that she could be still and think. She needed to sort out exactly what she was hoping for in this visit, apart from getting together with an aunt of whom she was fond. That in itself was one element, of course. Suddenly family seemed to have become more important to her.

I wonder why I've never really thought about trying to contact my father before? she mused. *Is it the fact that I'm gradually losing my mother or is it that the prospect of having my own children makes me more interested in my inheritance – to put it bluntly, my genes? Perhaps it's a mixture of both.*

She took out the photograph of her father again and studied it. A handsome man, young and fit-looking. *He won't look like that now,* she thought. *Why did he leave? Was it another woman, some problem like alcohol, did my mother drive him away? She could be difficult even before she was ill.*

No that's not fair, she chided herself, but then, her inner voice replied, *She could have given you an explanation. Was it fair of her to tell me and Pat nothing? I suppose she just wanted him to disappear out of our lives as if he had never been – especially when Ted came along. Aunt Sarah must know something, and perhaps she could even tell me something that would help me find him now. Sometimes other family members keep in touch after a divorce and she probably wouldn't tell Mum if she had.*

Thinking of her mother gave Stella the urge to phone Charlie for an update. She would miss her weekend visit and felt guilty about it. *I can't hand over responsibility for my mother to a robot.* And yet increasingly the temptation was to do exactly that. *Charlie is so competent,* she admitted to herself. *He knows exactly how to handle my mother and she adores him. She gives the impression of being pleased to see me, but I reckon she's forgotten I've been as soon as I've left, and I do struggle to find things to say to her. Trying to get any memories of my father out of her was hopeless. I wonder whether she even remembers now that she had children.*

Succumbing to the urge, Stella went out into the corridor, taking her phone with her, and dialled the number of her mother's flat. The rattle in the corridor was so great that she found herself shouting to make herself heard when the phone was answered.

Charlie's voice, however, came through with great clarity, although it was not loud. "Hello, Stella. I expect you're phoning for an update on your mother. You mustn't worry about missing a visit. Time really means nothing to your mother these days. She'll be just as pleased to see you when you get back."

This response to her greeting startled Stella, as she hadn't told Charlie or her mother that she was going away. "Um…" she hesitated, "I'm on a train."

"Yes," said Charlie simply, and Stella didn't feel inclined to explore further what he knew or had guessed about her plans.

"Yes, Charlie. I just wanted to check Mum was OK. I'm sorry I won't be able to get over this weekend. I'm going up to Edinburgh to visit my aunt."

"Everything's completely fine, Stella." Charlie's voice was perfectly calm. "Your mother did have rather a bad night last night, but she's perfectly OK now. She's sitting in the living room watching the children's programmes on television. She enjoys that, as you know."

Stella's voice rose. "Charlie, what do you mean by 'a bad night'?"

"I didn't phone you, Stella, because it was all over very quickly and it was the middle of the night. As I said, your mother is now completely fine."

"Please, Charlie." Stella spoke through gritted teeth, rigid with alarm and irritation. "Tell me exactly what happened."

"Of course, Stella. Well, your mother woke in quite a lot of pain, which does happen from time to time with her heart condition. She was distressed, but luckily, of course, I was at hand and was able to give her her medication and calm her down. She is quite comfortable now. Everything's under control, so please relax and enjoy your trip."

Stella found it difficult to keep her voice level. "I was completely unaware that this sort of thing was happening, Charlie. It sounds serious. I didn't know she was ever in pain. I want to be told about everything. So if it happens again you must phone me, day or night. Day or night, Charlie, is that clear?"

"That's absolutely clear Stella, and of course I'll do as you ask. But you must remember that I'm here all the time, and my only purpose is to look after your mother and make sure she is comfortable and happy."

"Yes, but *you* must understand, Charlie." Stella was shouting now over the noise of the train but also with a sense of panic and frustration that she could not control. "I'm her daughter; I'm family. Ultimately she's my responsibility, mine and my brother's."

"Of course I understand that, Stella," was the calm response. "But you can be absolutely confident that I will always act in your mother's best interests. That is my sole purpose. That is what I've been programmed to do."

I have the feeling that we're not always talking on the same wavelength, thought Stella, but she just said, "I'm going to ring off now, Charlie. I know what you're saying, but please let me know whenever anything like this happens. Otherwise I'll only worry."

"Of course, Stella. I really do hope you can enjoy your trip. We'll see you when you get back."

Concerned as Stella was about her mother and the uneasiness she felt about the degree of control that Charlie had over her mother, she found herself, as she always did on the train journey up the East Coast, gradually caught up in the beauty and excitement of the landscape. It really began at Newcastle where passengers looked across from the dizzy heights of the King Edward V11 railway bridge at the majestic parade of sister bridges spanning the mighty Tyne into the distance.

Then the landscape, already tougher than that in the lush South and Midlands but still green and patch-worked with arable fields, opened out to reveal large skies and sudden cliffs jutting out of the plains. And when the train curved round Berwick on Tweed, nestling within its mediaeval wall, the estuary patrolled by stately sea-going swans, Stella found her spirits rising despite herself. *It's good for me to get away for a bit*, she thought.

The sun came out, so by the time the line was running along next to the sea, Stella could enjoy the white-topped waves curling onto empty golden sands and put the telephone call with Charlie behind her. *It feels so much calmer, simpler up here*, she said to herself. *I wonder if Jem would consider leaving London? But could we find work? Perhaps I could, but it would be a problem for Jem. Scottish law is different.* She sighed and took out her phone to key her aunt's postcode into the street finder. Sarah had recently downsized to a flat in the New Town in a street which Stella did not know.

The train pulled into Edinburgh Waverley station and, with the sun still shining, Stella, with her small wheeled suitcase, made her way up the stairs to the walkway which spanned the station. Standing on the escalator which enabled travellers to by-pass a steep flight of steps up to Princes Street, she noted changes since she had last visited. Some of the old familiar shops alongside the steps had disappeared, leaving empty units. *It happens everywhere*, she thought. *Everything changes. I never used to notice.*

Waiting to cross the road, she turned, as she always did when she arrived in Edinburgh, to look at the skyline marking the path of the Royal Mile, like a set of jagged teeth silhouetted against what was today a clear sky. At the summit, the ancient grey solidity of the castle dominated the city, as it had done for centuries. *The best skyline in the world*, she thought.

Following her Waze, Stella crossed the road and, making her way through the cobbled alleyway of East Register Street, emerged into gracious St Andrew Square, with its stately Georgian buildings and manicured lawns. Her aunt's flat was in Dublin Street, which led directly off the square, part of the graceful grid that made up the Georgian part of the city. She smiled at the thought that the New Town, created as an escape for the well-to-do from the stench and squalor of the swamp now transformed into Princes Street Gardens, was more than 150 years old. *But everything was new once,* she reminded herself. *Perhaps one day even robots will seem historic.*

Halfway down Dublin Street, she found her aunt's building and rang the bell marked 'McLeod'. It was one of three bells for flats that appeared to share one graceful front door topped by a spider's web fanlight.

Aunt Sarah's voice came through over the entry phone. "Stella, is that you? Come on up." And with a buzz the door came off the latch.

Stella pulled her case into a narrow flagged hall with three doors opening off it. The one facing her now opened to reveal her aunt, who came out into the hall to give her a hug.

"Lovely to see you," she said fondly. "Come in, come in – but before you do, just look up."

And Stella, having hugged her aunt back, dutifully looked up to see that the ceiling, painted Wedgewood blue, was covered with a fine white tracery of moulding like the most delicate icing or lace.

"Aunt Sarah," she gasped, "it's exquisite."

"Wait till you see the flat," responded Sarah. "I'm thrilled with it."

She took hold of Stella's case and led her through the door from which she had appeared and up a curving staircase, painted the same Wedgewood blue as the hall to a grand landing along which a richly coloured Turkish runner had been laid to soften the granite flagstones.

"I've got the main rooms of what was the townhouse," she said. "That's why they're so large, and I've got an Adam fireplace – look." And she showed Stella into a huge room, dominated by a large sash window and elaborate fire mantel painted white. "I'm afraid this is my room," she said. "You're in here, but it's still pretty good, isn't it?" She showed Stella into a smaller, but still spacious, room next door. "Your bathroom is across the landing. I have my own."

"It's fantastic," gasped Stella, "and you're so close to Princes Street and George Street and all the shops and restaurants."

"It's perfect for me," Sarah replied, "although I might find toiling up the hill a bit much when I get older. But at the moment it's perfect," she repeated. "After Alastair died, I didn't need all those bedrooms and I wanted to be nearer in."

Alastair McLeod had died two years before. He had been the reason that Sarah had moved to Scotland in the first place, and she and Alastair had lived in Edinburgh for the whole of their married lives. When Alastair died, Sarah had considered moving back to Southern England, nearer to her roots and what family she had left. But when it came to it, having been a teacher in Edinburgh for many years, and having been married for so long to a Scot, she had found that she had come to regard Edinburgh as home and decided to stay. Stella and her brother had been delighted to continue to have an excuse to visit the city – and a place to stay, although now he had a child it would not be so easy for Patrick to visit often.

"I want to hear all about everything. All about Jem, and Patrick's little one – and about Christine, of course. But I'll let you freshen up and settle in first. If you want a lie down, that's fine. I'll bring you a cup of tea?"

"I don't need a lie down, Aunt Sarah," was Stella's response, "but a cup of tea would be lovely."

Later, in the pale blue dusk, which at this time of year lasted until at least 9pm, Sarah and Stella walked along the cobbled 'meuse' at the side of the building which housed Sarah's flat and into Northumberland Street. The street was lit by tall, flower-like Victorian lamps and oblongs of light from unshuttered windows, many on the lower floors, to Stella's fascination, disclosing grand chandeliers and rooms painted in rich ochres and reds rarely used in London houses. Much higher up some of the smaller windows under the eaves revealed humbler light fittings, round paper light shades. *Like little moons*, Stella thought.

"This is so beautiful," said Stella, wondering once again why she lived in London.

"I love it," said Sarah, leading Stella towards a welcoming doorway from which emanated a comfortable buzz of conversation and the odd clink of glass. "And this is my favourite pub."

The Cumberland Arms was a Victorian pub with a long bar and a number of side rooms and snugs.

Sarah ushered Stella into one of these, a narrow space with a long table and bench seating for about eight people around the sides.

"We can be private in here – for the time being, at any rate," she said, settling Stella in.

While Sarah was away getting the drinks, Stella checked her phone. There was a message from Jem so she must call him soon, but to her relief nothing from Charlie.

Sarah came back with two small glasses of a pale gold liquid. "I know you're not a big fan, but do try this one. I think you may like it and you really ought to sample the local produce. It's a single malt, a speyside. It has almost a scented taste. Anyway, if you don't, I'll take it and get you something else."

Stella took a tentative sip and said, "Actually it's very nice. Don't take it away."

Sarah settled herself down on the bench next to Stella and said, "I have a feeling there's a purpose to this visit, Stella. Not that it's not great to have you here, but you don't usually come up at such short notice – and it's been a while as well. It can't be about Christine. From what you said on the phone she's well looked after at the moment. We're pretty private in here – go on, fire away."

"You're absolutely right, of course," responded Stella. "I guess something was sparked off for me by Mum starting to lose it – it's as if she's drifting away from me. And then, Jem and me getting engaged started me thinking about the children we might have. And my mother dug out some old photographs."

"You're going to ask me about your father, I think, aren't you Stella?" Sarah looked at Stella's face and then into her whisky.

"Yes. That's what it's all about." Stella opened her bag and took out the photograph of her father. "I rescued this from Mum's collection. In fact, I rescued the whole lot. The robot brought them out. He seemed to know that she might destroy them, and she did suddenly seem to get upset as we were going through them. I really think she might have done it if he hadn't given them to me to take away."

"Yes, I've heard of that happening," said Sarah. "I've actually given a lot of mine to Bob already. I want to ask you more about the robot later. The set-up sounds unbelievably futuristic. I can't imagine what it's like to experience, but I suppose if it works it's one answer to a very difficult problem."

She took the photograph from Stella. "Yes, that's David all right. What a handsome man he was."

"Why did they split up?" asked Stella. "Mum just wouldn't talk about it, and anyway, Patrick and I didn't want to upset her by asking."

"It was drink, really," said Sarah, "not women, although there was a bit of that as well – later on. Christine threw him out in the end. He paid some maintenance for a bit and then seemed to disappear. In fact, he'd taken a job overseas – somewhere in the Emirates, I think."

"So you must have had some sort of contact after he left," Stella said hopefully.

"Not for quite a few years, but then – I don't know how he found me, because by this time I was married to Alastair and living in Edinburgh – he suddenly turned up on our doorstep." She paused and put her hand on Stella's, which was resting on the table touching the photograph.

"He was terribly changed. I wouldn't have recognised him. I'm sorry, Stella, I know you're hoping that you might be able to get in touch with him now, but he came to see me because he was dying. He had cancer and it was very obvious that he hadn't long to go. He wanted to know what had happened to you all, but especially to you and Patrick. I showed him some photographs and he took one away with him. I got the impression he hadn't had any more children, although I didn't ask him. I left him to tell me if he wanted to and didn't volunteer any information about you three. I felt sorry for him, seeing him like that, but I didn't feel we owed him anything. I did tell him that Christine had remarried, happily. I think that had an effect on him. He left saying he would come back the next day, but he never came back. I'm sorry, Stella, but I'm sure he's dead."

"How long ago was this?" said Stella, conscious of an unexpectedly painful sense of disappointment.

"Well, about fifteen years ago. You'd have been about eighteen and Patrick just still at university. I knew Christine wouldn't want to be told, and I did think about telling you and Patrick privately, but there didn't seem any point in stirring things up and upsetting everyone. And Ted was such a great father to you both."

"Yes, he was," said Stella quietly. And then after a pause, "Do you mind if I just go outside to call Jem? I should have phoned him earlier but got distracted by looking at the flat and talking to you. And I'd like to tell him about my dad."

"Of course," said Sarah, picking up Stella's glass. "Another of those?"

Stella smiled as she pushed her way out from behind the table. "No thanks. It was very nice, but I think I'll have a whisky mac this time – a proper one with ginger wine."

"OK," Sarah laughed, "but it'll be blended for you. I'm not putting a single malt into ginger wine."

Outside in the darkening street, Stella stood under a street lamp and dialled Jem's number. She felt a surge of relief when she heard his voice say, "Hi there. How's it going? I'm missing you."

"Oh, and me too," she said, but quietly, as there were drinkers sitting at tables nearby. She got straight to the point. "I've asked Aunt Sarah about Dad, and... and..." her voice cracked a little, "it's no go. He's almost certainly dead."

"Oh," Jem's voice was gentle, "I'm so sorry, darling. But I guess it was always likely."

"I know that really," said Stella, "and I never thought about it before now. It must have been finding that photo." *And thinking about having children with you.*

"I think it's your mother's condition too, isn't it?" Jem said gently. "You feel you're losing her."

"I do, you're right. And it's not just the dementia. I feel that damned robot is more important to her than I am. He's the one she asks for all the time."

"Don't get it out of proportion, love. He's just a machine – remember what Hod says. He's the expert, so think of it as being like a medicine or... or a life-support machine. It's what she needs at the moment."

"I'll try. I'm sorry. I'm being silly."

Stella could hear background voices down the phone and she knew from the slight breathlessness in his voice that Jem was walking as he was talking.

"Are you out?"

"I'm just walking to the Tesco local to pick up some milk and other stuff. Sorry, I should have stopped. There, I've stopped now."

"It's OK. I have to go back in, anyway. Aunt Sarah's waiting. She's got a great flat. We're going to do some nice things tomorrow. We have to come up sometime."

"I'd love that. Perhaps we could grab a few days during the Festival – if your aunt wouldn't mind, that is. I'd like to get to know her." Jem paused. "Look, I know you've had a disappointment, but I think it's good for you to get away. Try and relax, and don't worry about your mum. Charlie and I can cope very well without you."

Should I tell him about the phone call? Stella wondered but decided that there was no point. There was nothing that Jem could do. *Mum's my responsibility, not his.*

"Well, it is great to get some time with Aunt Sarah and I do love Edinburgh. She wants to meet you too," said Stella. "I've told her all about you and I know she's pleased I'm getting settled. She's going to love you."

"Well, hopefully you'll have given me a good write-up," laughed Jem. "Look – off you go back in. Have a nice day tomorrow. At least you may be able to find out a bit more about your dad before you come home and you can get some good shopping in on George Street."

"Yes, that's for sure – but I'm looking forward to being back. I'm missing you. Love you."

"Love you too," was the fond response, and Stella ended the call, turning back towards the lighted doorway of the pub.

Before she had gone back inside, however, her phone rang.

He's forgotten something, she thought. But when she answered it was not Jem's voice she heard but Charlie's coming through with a strange clarity, almost as if he were inside her own head.

"I'm sorry to interrupt your visit, Stella." Charlie's manner was calm but serious.

"Charlie," she said sharply, "there's nothing wrong is there? I mean, with Mum."

"Your mother is safe and in good hands," was the reply, "but I thought you'd want me to tell you we've had to take her into hospital. She's had what I think you might describe as 'a bit of a turn.'"

"Hospital." Stella's voice rose shrilly. "What's happened? Oh, God – why am I not there?"

"You really don't need to worry, Stella." The continuing calmness of Charlie's voice made Stella want to scream. "These episodes will tend to happen with Christine's condition, but they can be dealt with in hospital. She's had little intervals of faintness from time to time, but this was more serious, so I asked the Whittington to admit her. She's perfectly comfortable now."

Stella found it impossible to keep the panic and a degree of resentment from her voice. "You've never told me that she's been having 'incidents' like that. I'll come back immediately. I'm sure I can get a train to get me back to London tonight."

"There's really no need to do that, Stella. Your mother's very comfortable now and I can be with her on the ward in case she wakes."

"It's *my* mother, Charlie." Stella found herself talking to Charlie through gritted teeth for the second time that day. "And I want to be with her. I'll get the first train I can. Please text details of the ward." And with that, she ended the call and fled back inside to her aunt.

CHAPTER
FORTY-ONE

By the time Stella and her aunt had collected Stella's things and got her back to the station, it was ominously empty.

"I'm afraid you may have missed the last regular train," said Sarah. "You might still get the sleeper as it's mid-week, but you won't get much sleep unless you get a cabin, which is terribly expensive. Why not stay until tomorrow? Then you can have a good night's sleep and still be there by lunch time."

"I won't get any sleep anyway, Auntie," was the reply. And, leaving her case with her aunt, Stella crossed the deserted ticket hall to the solitary desk which remained open.

From a distance it had appeared that the desk was manned, but as she got closer, Stella realised that what appeared to be the desk window was in fact a screen. Beside it was a button with the notice 'Please press for assistance' displayed beside it.

Stella pressed and a face appeared on the screen.

"How can I help?" the face asked, and Stella realised at once that she was in effect speaking to a machine as she said, "I need to get to London tonight. It's very urgent and I don't mind what it costs."

The face, which was female with a bland regularity of feature which Stella had come to associate with robots, smiled and assured her, "I'll see what is available. The regular services have ceased for the night."

"I'm aware of that. I thought I might be able to get onto the sleeper." Stella tried to keep her voice under control and stay calm. There was no point in trying to pressurise a machine.

"I'm just checking for you now," the face responded without in any way changing expression or position.

There was a pause.

"There is a place available on the sleeper train which leaves from platform two in ten minutes. It's only a reclining seat. All the cabins are taken. Do you want to reserve that?"

"That's fine," said Stella, panicking slightly at the short time frame available to get herself and her luggage onto the train. "How do I pay?" She couldn't see any sort of card machine on her side of the counter and the screen completely covered the aperture in the glass partition which fronted the counter.

"Just place the face of your card against this screen," was the reply. "Thank you. I'm printing your ticket now. It will be issued from the dispenser in front of you below this counter." And as the face spoke some type of machinery stirred into life in front of Stella at waist level and her ticket appeared with a receipt.

"Thank you," she said, grabbing both, despite the fact that she knew she was addressing a machine.

The voice followed her out of the ticket hall. "You're very welcome. Have a good journey."

Stella did not have a good journey, but then she had not expected to have one. She always found it difficult to sleep in the presence of strangers, so the fact that she could stretch out on the reclining seat was really no help. Also, her thoughts were in turmoil.

As she stared at her own reflection in the black glass of the train window, she found herself going over and over the same questions. How serious was her mother's condition? Why had she, Stella, not been told about it, or if she had been told, why had she not been told in such a way as to make her understand the seriousness of it? Was there any chance that she might arrive too late and find her mother dead? At the bottom of all these worries was a deep feeling of guilt. Was it right to have handed over prime responsibility for her mother to a robot? She also came to realise that although she had thought she had come to terms with her mother's gradual drift into mental oblivion, she had not in any way come to terms with the idea of her death.

She must have slept fitfully but was wide awake as the train pulled into Euston in the thin morning light. Cold and stiff, she hurried along the platform with her small wheeled case and down the stairs to the subterranean taxi rank.

She needed to be taken straight to the hospital door. The underground might not yet be running.

The taxi dropped her at the hospital entrance. Like the station, the hospital seemed eerily empty, although it was clear that activity among the staff had begun and there was a smell of food in the air. On reaching the ward, Stella was greeted by a nurse who had an air of authority.

"You must be Stella. We've been expecting you. I'm Staff Nurse Pritchard and I'm one of the nurses in charge of your mother's care. Can we just have a word before I take you to see your mother?"

"Yes, I'm Christine Mayfield's daughter," said Stella as she followed the nurse into a small glassed-in office from which the entire length of the ward was visible. She could see Charlie farther down the ward sitting next to one of the beds.

"Do sit down," Staff Nurse Pritchard said in a voice which managed to combine sympathy with authority. "Your mother is quite comfortable now, Stella and, as you probably know, her carer, who came in with her in the ambulance, has been with her all night."

"Yes, I did know that the *robot* had come with her," replied Stella, brutally emphasising the word 'robot'. *Let's not pretend that this is a person – and don't spare me the thought that it should have been me.*

"Well, Stella," was the calm response, "I know you're concerned about your mother – that's very natural – but you can be reassured. Her condition is completely stable now. She's not in any danger. However, it was right for the carer to bring her in when he did."

"I'm sorry I wasn't nearer at hand when it happened," said Stella. "I'll be honest with you" – *Might as well*, she thought – "I don't feel comfortable leaving all these big decisions to a robot."

"That's very understandable," Nurse Pritchard acknowledged. "Many of my staff have had similar concerns. You may not have noticed on your way up, but this hospital now has a small number of robots engaged in routine patient care. It's very much early days, but I think we can be very confident that using robots in this way is going to be part of everyone's care in the future."

"I didn't know," said Stella, trying to think back to the staff she had seen as she made her way into the building.

"I just wanted to reassure you about your mother's condition," Nurse Pritchard said, getting up from her chair with an indication that Stella should do the same. "And I wanted to alert you to the fact that one of the helpers who will be assisting with your mother's day-to-day needs on the ward will be a robot – rather like Charlie. I find it's best to warn people what to expect. If you're able to wait until after breakfast, the registrar will be round and he can answer any detailed questions you have about your mother's condition and treatment."

Stella found that all she could think of to say in response to this was, "Thank you. I didn't know these robots were being used in hospital," her heart sinking a little. "There's no problem about me waiting," she went on. "I can stay as long as necessary. I'm not working this week," she continued as she followed Nurse Pritchard down the ward to where Charlie was sitting.

As she got closer, Stella could see that her mother was wide awake, albeit lying back on the pillows. Christine and Charlie appeared to be having a quiet conversation.

It's ridiculous to feel jealous, thought Stella, but she had to admit she did.

"Hello, Mum," she said briskly, coming to the head of the bed to kiss her mother and ignoring Charlie.

As was often the case, her mother looked momentarily confused before replying with her usual greeting. "Hello dear."

Stella had long since ceased to speculate as to whether her mother remembered who she was when she first appeared, although she was pretty sure that, as her visits progressed, some memories did genuinely come back to her.

"Hello, Stella." Charlie's voice was quiet, deferential. "I hope you managed to get some sleep on the train."

"Not really Charlie," was the brusque reply, "but it's fine. I'm not working this week, so I can catch up." She paused before adding, grudgingly, "Thank you for phoning me last night."

"I was sorry to spoil your trip, Stella, but I knew you would want to be kept informed."

"I'm not sure why I'm here," Christine cut in plaintively. "I can't remember how I got here. I was at home and then suddenly I was here. Thank goodness Charlie was with me."

"Yes, Mum, thank goodness." And Stella had to admit to herself the truth of that statement. "I'll be talking to the doctor soon and finding out when you can go home."

"I believe Christine will be able to go home today," Charlie said.

Stella tried to keep the irritation she felt at this intervention out of her voice. "Yes, well. According to the staff nurse I'll be able to speak to the registrar later so then I'll be able to find out…" she paused, "officially."

"Of course you'd like to speak to the registrar, Stella. I understand," Charlie said, and then, as if to relieve the tension that had crept into the exchanges between himself and Stella, "I believe the nurse will be round in a few minutes to do the routine checks and make Christine's bed. Ah – here she comes now." And he turned towards the entrance to the ward where a nurse was pushing a trolley towards them.

Stella turned to look and for a moment was lost for words. It was clear, even from a distance, that the figure coming towards them in the uniform of a junior nurse was a robot. The smoothness of carriage, the regularity of face and figure were, to Stella's mind, inhuman.

Having performed her duties at neighbouring beds, the nurse wheeled her trolley to a stop next to Christine. Conversation around the bed had died during the wait, so her arrival was something of a relief to Stella.

"You must be Stella." The nurse greeted her with a radiant smile. "Your mother will be so pleased to have you with her. I am Nurse Roberts, and Christine and I are just getting to know each other, aren't we, Christine? How are you feeling this morning?"

Stella's mother replied with an answering beam. "Very well, thank you, dear. But I'd really like to go home."

Stella noticed that Charlie and Nurse Roberts did not acknowledge each other or interact visibly in any way, which would have been odd if they'd both been human. Despite the lack of verbal connection, however, she had the strange impression that they were in communication with each other in some way. *Not possible. Don't be silly*, she said to herself. *And anyway, why would they acknowledge each other? There's no reason to if they're were both machines?*

"I think you'll be able to go home later today," Nurse Roberts said to Christine soothingly.

"That's for the doctor to decide, surely," said Stella, almost rudely.

Nurse Roberts turned to her with a smile and said gently, "Of course, Stella. The doctor is in charge. Always." She paused and continued, "I'm just going to change Christine's bed now and then breakfast will be served, so if you'd like to go away and get some breakfast yourself, Stella, by the time you come back you should catch the doctor on his rounds."

"OK," said Stella reluctantly, although she did admit to herself that she was hungry. "I assume Charlie won't be staying either."

Nurse Roberts now turned towards Charlie for the first time but said nothing.

"Yes, I'll go and wait somewhere else," Charlie said. "It will give more room for the bedmaking and the trolley."

But he's only doing it to humour me, thought Stella. *The nurse wouldn't mind his staying here. At least he realises I don't want to sit with him while I eat breakfast. I wonder how they program in that sort of intuition.*

Anxious to ensure that she avoided Charlie's company during the break, Stella gave her mother a quick peck on the cheek. "See you in a bit, Mum. Enjoy your breakfast." And she made her way quickly out of the ward.

CHAPTER
FORTY-TWO

As both Charlie and Nurse Roberts had predicted, Christine was allowed home that day.

The registrar had explained to Stella that her mother was liable to suffer small strokes from time to time but that these could largely be controlled by medication and that Charlie was competent to take the necessary action to mitigate their effects. It should normally be possible to avoid hospital admission, but in this case the robot had made the correct judgement in bringing her to hospital.

"These small strokes will probably continue to contribute to the decline in your mother's cognitive function," he explained. "But the latest medication is very effective, and with the twenty-four-hour care that the robot can provide, we can hopefully continue to support your mother in her own home for some time."

Well, no one can say that they are giving me false hope, thought Stella as she went back to the ward to find that Charlie and Christine, fully dressed and clearly ready to leave, were waiting for her.

Although she knew the answer, Stella asked, "Are all her things packed up?"

"Everything's ready, Stella, and the ambulance is waiting outside to take us back. I have the new medication. I can explain the instructions for administration when we get to the flat."

Why bother? was Stella's thought. *It won't involve me at all.* But she merely said, "Thank you, Charlie. Can you bring the case, please?"

On their way out, they passed Nurse Roberts. "Goodbye, Christine," she said with her charming smile. "I'm just going off-duty. It's been a pleasure looking after you. Goodbye, Stella, take care and try not to worry. Christine is in good hands."

Once again she and Charlie made no acknowledgement of each other, although Nurse Roberts stood back to allow Charlie to wheel the case past her.

I suppose we'll all have to get used to this, Stella said to herself. *But I'm not sure I can.*

The ambulance pulled up on the double yellow lines outside the door to Christine's flat and the cheery young paramedic jumped out of the front passenger seat to open the doors and help Stella and Christine out. He clearly felt that Charlie had no need of assistance.

"I'll open up if you bring Mum and her bag inside, Charlie," said Stella, taking the lead.

As she entered the narrow, dark hall, Stella nearly tripped over Cadbury, who jumped back with a loud complaint.

"Cadbury," she said, stooping to stroke him. "Have you been waiting for Mummy?" But Cadbury backed away from her hand and padded slowly towards the kitchen.

"I'll feed you in a minute," Stella told him and turned to guide her mother into the living room.

"Come and sit down, Mum, I'll make a nice cup of tea for us. Cadbury's pleased to see us, I think," she said, ushering her mother towards her favourite armchair. The living room windows faced south and the room was flooded with noonday sunlight.

"Cadbury?" her mother said questioningly.

"Yes, you know, Cadbury, your cat." Stella tried to keep the impatience out of her voice.

"Oh, yes dear," her mother responded, settling herself into the chair. "A cup of tea would be lovely."

"I can do that for you, Stella." Charlie's voice came soft but penetrating from the bedroom where he was unpacking Christine's case without being asked. The flat was immaculate.

"It's all right, Charlie." Stella's response was firm. "I can do it. I want to." *And I want to check out what's happening in the kitchen*, she said to herself. However, if she had thought she would be able to fault Charlie's arrangements in any way, she was disappointed. The kitchen was tidy and sparkling clean, the store cupboard well stocked with tea, sugar and biscuits, and the fridge with fresh milk.

Stella put the kettle on, laid out a tea tray and turned to Cadbury, who was waiting quietly beside his bowl.

Now where's the cat food? she asked herself, but she didn't want to have to consult Charlie, so she dug around until she found it in the cupboard under the sink. She ladled a generous amount into Cadbury's bowl and he fell on it with uncharacteristic voracity. He was now a very old cat, and as he had aged his appetite had diminished to a degree that had worried Stella in the past. Because of the amount of fur he carried, he looked enormous, but when Stella lifted him up nowadays he felt incredibly light, his delicate bones prominent beneath the fur.

However, by the time she had finished making the tea, Cadbury had cleared his bowl and was at her feet asking for more.

"This is not like you, Cadbury," Stella said. "I'm not sure you should have any more just now." She was aware that recently there had been incidents of Cadbury being sick in various parts of the flat. In one case she had inadvertently stood in a little pile of vomit in her mother's bedroom.

She stooped to pick him up, noting again how fragile he felt under his fur.

"I'll take you through to Mum. She'd like to see you." And she began to carry him through to the living room. But as she did so she felt something under his ribs.

She settled Cadbury on her mother's lap and returned for the tea tray, saying as she did so, "Could you just come and help me in the kitchen for a minute, Charlie?"

When Charlie appeared, she closed the door and, keeping her voice low, said, "I think I'd better take Cadbury to the vet, Charlie. There seems to be a lump down by his ribs."

As in most situations, Charlie's reaction was a model of calm. "I had noticed that, Stella, and was intending to alert you to it once we had dealt with your mother's condition. I'm afraid that Cadbury has a cancerous tumour on one of his kidneys. Of course, he is very old for a cat, and cats as a species do tend to have problems with their kidneys as they age."

"That's as may be," Stella responded tartly, "but I'll need to have him looked over by a vet. As you know, my mother's devoted to him. She'll be devastated if there's anything seriously wrong."

"Of course, I understand that you want Cadbury to be seen by a specialist, Stella. But I don't think you need to worry about your mother. She enjoys Cadbury while he is there, but I believe she forgets about him when he is not. I am confident that once he had gone she would not notice his absence."

"There's no question of Cadbury being 'gone', as you put it," said Stella. "My mother has pet insurance cover and whatever it costs to treat Cadbury will be done. If you'll stay here, I'll dig out the cat basket and take him to the vet down the road this afternoon."

"I know exactly where the cat basket is," was Charlie's response. "I'll get it for you. I'm sorry this is so upsetting for you. Of course, when there is no hope of recovery sometimes it is in the best interests of an animal not to prolong the suffering. I believe Cadbury is suffering now. He is in pain."

Stella was too irritated by this speech to reply and turned away to fetch her coat and collect Cadbury from his perch on her mother's lap.

"We won't be long, Mum," she said, scooping up the cat who made a faint sound of protest, but he submitted with uncharacteristic docility. "I'm just taking Cadbury to the vet. He needs some medicine."

"Oh, thank you dear," her mother said, rearranging her skirt. "I hope he's all right." But she did not seem unduly worried. "Ah, there's the tea," she continued, beaming as Charlie came in with the tray. "Just what I wanted."

And Stella, having deposited Cadbury with surprising ease into the cat basket which Charlie had left in the hall, let herself quietly out of the front door.

It was two hours before Stella returned to the flat. She let herself in with her key and put the cat basket down in the hall. It was empty.

After a long wait in the company of an assortment of animals and their owners, Stella had finally managed to get in to see the vet.

The young woman had taken Cadbury out of the basket and felt him all over with great gentleness before turning to Stella and saying, "I'm afraid Cadbury has cancer. He has a large tumour on one of his kidneys and the cancer seems to have spread to his stomach. Have you noticed any change in his eating pattern? He will be finding it hard to take in enough nutrition."

Stella had felt a stronger stab of grief at this news than she would have thought possible. Cadbury had been a feature of family life for the past eighteen years. It was many years since she had lived with him and her mother, but he was still a symbol of home to her. He seemed always to have been part of the family although he had had predecessors.

"He doesn't live with me; he lives with my mother," she had said, her voice a little unsteady. "I did notice today that he seemed to be voraciously hungry – which is unusual for him."

"Yes," was the response. "He can't digest food efficiently anymore. And, you know, he's in pain. I know this is difficult for you, but I think the time has come for you to ask yourself whether it is fair to him to keep him going in this condition."

"Oh no." Stella felt the tears coming. "Surely there must be something we can do."

"I have to be honest with you," the vet had said. "If we let this go on, we are prolonging Cadbury's suffering. Is that really fair – to him or to your mother?" She paused. "I can give you some time to think about it in the waiting room if you need it, but really the kindest thing we could do is to end it now with an injection. You can hold him while I do it. It will be as if he is going to sleep in your arms."

And Stella, the scientist, had had to accept the absolute logic of this. She had held Cadbury on her knee while the vet gave him the injection, and he went limp in her arms while tears streamed down her face.

She had dreaded returning to the flat without Cadbury, but of course her mother had forgotten that she had taken him out. Charlie and her mother were watching a children's programme on television. Charlie rose to give Stella his seat next to Christine, but Stella waved him back. He remained standing, however, and said, "Can I help you with anything, Stella?"

Christine, absorbed in the programme, barely registered Stella's arrival. *Perhaps she doesn't remember I was going out,* Stella thought.

She said quietly to Charlie, "Can we just have a word in the corridor Charlie?" And Charlie followed her out of the room.

"Of course you were right," she told him dully. "It was cancer and the vet advised that he should be put down to save him further suffering."

"Yes, Stella," Charlie replied quietly. "I'm sure you've done the right thing. This was the best you could do for Cadbury. It's the role of the carer to make these hard decisions. You took the right course of action for Cadbury's welfare."

For once, Stella didn't respond with irritation. "I know you're right, Charlie. It was the best thing I could do, for Cadbury."

FORTY-THREE

"Can we have a cat when we get our house?" Stella leaned back against Jem, raised her face to the sun and stretched out her arms. She was lying between Jem's legs on a sunlounger which they had taken out onto the flat roof at the top of the building. Jem had been trying to read a newspaper, holding it at the end of an outstretched arm but now abandoned the attempt, throwing the paper down and putting his arms around her.

"I'm a dog person really," he said, burying his face in her neck.

"Oh dear," she mocked, "we're incompatible. There are dog people and cat people and never the twain shall meet. How can we possibly live together?"

"I should imagine," said Jem, removing his support and swivelling round to sit on the side of the lounger, "that we'll manage it by my giving in and agreeing to have a cat."

Stella sat up and smiled with the confidence of a woman who knows she is loved.

"I will make you love cats. It's just that you don't know them. Remember how gorgeous Cadbury was."

"He was certainly a character," was the guarded response. "I suppose they're less work than dogs and we do both have full-time jobs. I can't see myself getting up at 5.00am to walk a dog if I'm honest. But then, do we absolutely have to have an animal – from the get-go?"

"A home doesn't feel like a home to me without an animal," Stella said. *Or without a child*, she thought but didn't say. *Mum's flat feels sort of sterile to me now Cadbury's gone. The only link with what was home to me in the past is Mum – or what's left of her.*

Jem moved closer and put his hand on her shoulder. "I know it's very hard for you what's happening to your mother. In some ways I think it's worse than if she dies suddenly like my parents."

"Yes, it's hard, but I very much don't want her to die. There's enough left of what was Mum to make me want her to keep going. The doctors say that provided we look after her heart condition and arteries she could have years left. She's very strong otherwise."

"That's why it's so great to have Charlie," said Jem, getting up and gathering the paper together. "If Christine had a human carer you'd always be worried about what was going on when you weren't there, but with a carer robot you know that it will have been programmed always to put the wellbeing of the patient first – at least that's what Hod tells us and I believe him."

"You know Hod's off to the States?" Stella got up to follow Jem, who had folded the lounger and was carrying it indoors. "He phoned me at work last week. I forgot to say."

"Can't say I'm surprised," was the response. "Perhaps his accent will finally match his domicile."

"I'll miss him," said Stella thoughtfully. "He's a character, and it's so great to be able to get technical advice about robots. None of us laymen really has a clue about them or most of the AI we use. And it's everywhere now. Don't you think there should be more public discussion about how it's used? It's just crept up on us, hasn't it? It's everywhere. We really don't know now what's controlled by AI or algorithms or whatever and what's not anymore. No one's ever asked us – I mean, we ordinary people – whether we want it."

"You worry about it a lot more than I do," said Jem good-humouredly, starting to take out pans for the preparation of supper. "It's salmon tonight. Do you want to choose a bottle? I suppose it's having Charlie around which makes you think about this kind of stuff more than most people."

Stella chose a bottle from the fridge and started digging around in the cutlery drawer for a corkscrew. "You're right. And I guess that part of my feeling is almost jealousy because Mum seems to care more for Charlie than for me. I'm not sure she'd notice now if I never went, but she gets anxious if Charlie is out of the room for more than a few minutes. She can get very upset and frightened these days. I suppose it's not being able to make sense of things when she's having one of her 'turns.'"

"Look, my darling." Jem finished wrapping the salmon pieces in foil and slid them into the oven. He came over to

Stella and put his arms round her again. "Things will get more difficult with your mother and I'm afraid the sad truth is her quality of life is going to go on deteriorating. It's just something we're going to have to cope with. But you know you've always got me and I'm sure together we'll manage to cope."

"Yes, I know," she said. "I'm very lucky."

In the weeks and months that followed, Stella found house-hunting and planning her future with Jem a welcome distraction from concerns about her mother whose dementia continued to advance. Small things could provoke a reaction of extreme distress, even hostility towards Stella or even Charlie, although Charlie was extremely good at calming her down and dealing with Christine's gradual physical decline. *Much better than I am*, thought Stella, who began to feel more and more superfluous to her mother's needs. In a way this was liberating but also sad.

I've handed over the responsibility to Charlie, she would say to herself with a pang of guilt, which would be quickly submerged by the excitement of house viewings, ring buying and wedding plans. Jem had finally broached the question of a date. The date chosen was more than a year away, but planning and preparations were already in hand.

"That's the way it is nowadays," she explained to a baffled Jem. "These venues get booked up years in advance." And he submitted to the consequences of this analysis without protest, although he took little part in any of the active preparations.

The house hunt was problematic, as even with a relatively healthy budget it had confirmed that a house in Crouch End was out of their reach and they must move further out of London to find what they were looking for.

"We have to be near enough for you to be able to keep up your visits to your mother." To Stella's relief, Jem was very clear about that.

After a long search, they had managed to find a three-bedroomed house with garden in the less fashionable suburb of East Barnet which was still within relatively easy reach of Christine's flat and had good communications to their places of work.

So it was in the middle of a period of hectic activity and excited planning for the future that the call which Stella had long been dreading came.

It came not from Charlie but from an unknown female voice. "Am I speaking to Stella Mayfield?"

"Yes, I'm Stella Mayfield, who is this?" Stella, who had just arrived at work, turned away from her desk to take the call which had come in on her mobile.

"This is the Whittington Hospital here," the voice continued, "your mother, Christine Mayfield, has been admitted. We were given this number by your mother's carer."

"My mother? Oh no – what's happened?" Stella began immediately to gather up her things, signalling to her neighbour that she was about to leave.

"It's not appropriate to discuss this over the phone," the voice went on. "Are you able to come to the hospital straight away? Your mother's carer thought that you would be."

"I'm coming now. I can be there in forty minutes," Stella gasped in reply, holding the phone under her chin while she pulled on her jacket.

"As quickly as you can," was the response. "Ask for Ward 5."

When Stella presented herself to the nurses' station on Ward 5, it was clear that the nurse manning it was waiting for her.

"Please come with me, Stella," she said quietly, ushering Stella into a side office near the entrance doors. "Doctor Friedman will be here shortly to talk to you."

"I want to see my mother." Stella's voice rose in agitation. "Please can I see my mother?"

"I'm sorry, Stella, you can't see your mother at the moment. Please sit down and wait for the doctor. He won't be long. Let me get you a cup of tea."

"I don't want tea." Stella's voice continued to rise, in anger now, and she began to move towards the door. "I want to see my mother."

"You need to see the doctor first, Stella. Please sit down. I'll tell him you're here and I'm sure he'll get here as soon as he can. He realises how distressing this is for you," said the nurse, putting gentle pressure on Stella's shoulder and guiding her towards a chair facing a small desk.

Stella took out her phone and called Jem.

"I'm sorry, we don't allow phone calls on the ward," the nurse said apologetically, so Stella rose with the phone to her ear and went through the security doors onto the landing. She stood looking through the enormous glass window at the rooftops of North London, waiting for a response. The call went to voicemail. She then tried the number she had been given for Charlie. Charlie did not have a physical phone, but it was possible to communicate with him remotely by dialling what appeared to be a telephone number. There was no response to the call, something which had never happened before.

Stella went back onto the ward but did not sit down, intending to defy the nurse and go through to try to find her mother, but before she got to the door the doctor arrived.

He was breathless as if he had been running.

"Stella Mayfield?" he said, holding out his hand to Stella, who ignored it. "I'm Doctor Friedman. I was on duty when your mother was brought in by ambulance."

"Where is my mother?" Stella was aware that her voice had a note of hysteria. "What's happened?"

"Please sit down, Stella." Doctor Friedman continued to stand in front of the door, so Stella submitted and sat down, albeit on the edge of the chair.

Doctor Friedman took a seat behind a small desk opposite. "I'm very sorry to tell you, Stella, that we were unable to save your mother. She died early this morning. We tried to contact you on your mobile but couldn't get through."

"What?" Stella felt that she did not have enough breath to say more. Then, after a minute or two during which Doctor Friedman repeated that he was very, very sorry, she said, "What happened? What did she die of? The doctors have always said that her heart condition was well controlled. Was it a heart attack, a stroke?"

Doctor Friedman looked uncomfortable. "We are not sure of the exact cause of death yet, Stella. Your mother's carer called an ambulance in the early hours of this morning. I'm afraid your mother passed away before she reached us. Resuscitation was not possible."

Stella was overwhelmed by a sudden burst of dizziness and swayed on her chair. Doctor Friedman hurried from behind his desk to push her head between her knees and open the door to call for a nurse.

A nurse hurried in and bent over her with soothing words which Stella hardly registered.

"I know you'd like to see your mother, Stella, when you're feeling a little better. The nurse will bring you some tea with sugar in it. Please do try to drink it. It will help."

He stood irresolutely for a little while, clearly unsure of what to do next, before saying, "I'm going to leave you with Nurse Alam now, Stella, but I will be back to see you later and I'll try to answer any further questions you have, although, as I've said, there's not much more I can say at the moment. Can you take her into one of the side rooms, Nurse? I think number 2 is empty."

The nurse shepherded Stella into a small room and settled her on a chair next to a single bed. She sat and drank the strong, sweet tea that the nurse had brought her while the nurse, who was plump and middle-aged, sat next to her with an arm round her shoulder.

"Is Charlie here?" Stella asked when she had finished the tea. "The robot carer my mother had?"

"There's no one with your mother now, Stella. The robot was with your mother when she came in – he brought her in, of course. But I believe he's gone back to your mother's flat to sort some things out. At any rate, he's not here anymore."

"I need to speak to him." Stella realised how important this was to her. "It seems that he's the only one who knows what happened."

"He gave a full account when your mother was admitted," the nurse said. "It's all in the notes, but I'm afraid it doesn't tell us much about cause in itself. Your mother collapsed, Stella. The immediate cause was heart failure. I was not on duty when your mother was brought in."

"Who was?" Stella asked. "Can I speak to them?"

"Nurse Roberts was on ward duty when your mother came in, Stella, and Doctor Flack. They've both gone off-duty now, but I'm sure we can arrange for them to speak to you on another occasion."

"Did you say 'Nurse Roberts', the robot?" Stella felt panic rising.

"Yes, that's right, Nurse Roberts," Nurse Alam responded calmly, but there was a guardedness in her manner.

I'll never be at peace unless I speak to Charlie, thought Stella. *I must get back to the flat while he's still there.*

Consciously bracing herself, she stood up and said, "I'd like to see my mother now, please. Perhaps I could come back another time to talk to the doctor – with my fiancé."

"I think that's a very good idea, Stella." Nurse Alam, still kindly, was nevertheless clearly relieved that her role as comforter was coming to an end. "Follow me. We've put your mother in a side ward just down here." And she led the way out of the room.

CHAPTER
FORTY-FOUR

After leaving the hospital, Stella went straight to her mother's flat, a bare fifteen minutes' walk away.

She had never seen a dead body before, and it had been a shock to be confronted by her mother's body laid out on a hospital bed. The life had so clearly gone. *It's not my mother anymore*, she said to herself, looking at the strangely sunken, wax-like features. *Of course, they've taken her false teeth out – or Charlie did.* And that thought was somehow the most poignant of all. Her mother had always been so careful never to be seen without her false teeth – even as her dementia progressed. *Of course, Charlie must have helped her with putting them in*, Stella acknowledged to herself.

Having let herself into the flat, she found Charlie sitting, immobile, in the living room.

He rose as Stella came in. "I'm so glad to have seen you before I go, Stella."

"Go?" she said blankly.

"Yes. My job here is over, Stella. I have tried to make things as tidy as Christine would have liked and I hope that will be of some help to you, but I am due to be collected in a few minutes. I requested a little delay, as I knew you would want to speak to me."

"Yes, I need to speak to you, Charlie. I need to know exactly what happened. Why didn't you call me when my mother was taken ill like you did when I was in Scotland?" Stella tried to control it, but her voice gave away her anger.

"There isn't very much to tell, Stella." Charlie's voice was calm. "You wouldn't have been able to get here before Christine was taken to hospital. I can assure you that your mother did not suffer at all. I know that will have worried you."

"But what happened? She wasn't ill – well, not really. The doctors said her medication had her heart condition under control. She was still able to get about – well, a bit." Stella would have liked to have taken hold of Charlie and shaken him to make him answer, but as always, she was repelled by the idea of touching him, and anyway, it would have been pointless.

"I know this is difficult for you, Stella, but you know, your mother was not enjoying life anymore. Recently she had started to say to me that she wanted to die and, of course, we've known for a long time that she was on a steady downward path which could only end one way."

"That's not the point, Charlie." Stella was almost shouting. "Old people often say that sort of thing, and anyway, it doesn't explain why she would suddenly collapse. You say she didn't suffer," she said savagely. "How do you know?"

"You can be assured about that, Stella. I was with her when she passed away. She felt no pain at all. I didn't call you because she was gone by the time you could possibly have got here."

"But she wasn't really ill. There was no reason for her to die now. That's what I can't understand."

"Christine may have had other conditions, Stella." Charlie's voice was gentle and his facial expression sympathetic.

Stella sank down into a chair and put her head in her hands. *There's something he's not telling me*, she thought, *but I don't know how to get it out of him.*

"You may find," Charlie continued calmly, "that when the doctors have had more time to examine Christine they find something much more serious than the heart problem. Something like cancer, which could have resulted in a long-drawn-out and painful death. In that case, things would have become a lot worse for Christine very quickly. She would have suffered very much. This was really a much better outcome – for Christine and for you."

"What?" Stella's head snapped up. "Do you know something you haven't told me Charlie?" But as she spoke the doorbell rang.

Charlie moved into the corridor and towards the front door. "I have to go now, Stella. It has been a privilege to look after Christine and make her last months more comfortable, and I hope it has been a help to you also. You will now be able to proceed with your life without the constant worry about your mother's condition. And Christine is free of pain and anxiety."

He moved swiftly to the door and opened it.

Stella rushed into the corridor after him.

"Don't go yet – you can't. There are other things I need to know. Wait."

"I can't wait. As I said, my job here is done," Charlie said gently. "I am sure, Stella, that when you are able to think about these things calmly, you will come to an understanding of all I have done and appreciate the extent to which I have always put the welfare of my charge, Christine, and indeed of you yourself, before anything else. As my program requires. That is the way of robots."

And he turned and walked out of her life towards the technician who stood beside the open doors of a van, waiting for him.

 **Matador**

For exclusive discounts on Matador titles,
sign up to our occasional newsletter at
troubador.co.uk/bookshop